THE SHEIK OF ARABY

Lavinia Angell

Printed in the United States of America
First Printing: May 2010

ISBN-10: 1-45283-536-5
ISBN-13: 978-1-45283-536-5

Author's Note

A great debt is obviously owed to Jane Austen and E. M. Hull for the creation of the characters and settings used in this novel. This book attempts to blend the two works on which it is based, and in doing so retains many of the themes and bygone attitudes contained therein. It has never been the intention of the author to offend or generalize, and it is her hope that this work will be enjoyed in the spirit in which it was meant.

To Edith and Jane, in humble gratitude for their heroes.

To all those who encouraged me and aided in the creation of this book.

Lastly to Dave, my hero.

THE SHEIK OF ARABY

Pride and Prejudice in the Desert

A Novel by Lavinia Angell

Chapter 1

The hot midday air of Biskra was redolent with the spices of the East. To Elizabeth Bennet inhalation was happiness itself; filling her lungs with the unaccustomed mix heralded the new sensation and brought all its alien charm into her body. Her every fiber thrummed with the emotion, the noise of the place, which was foreign and jarring but indescribably thrilling. For an Englishwoman in a strange land, each new sensation was a discovery. Leaning out of the carriage, Elizabeth closed her eyes and listened. A merchant ring a gong until it became merely one long clang of market call, and the incomprehensible Arabic chatter of the natives as they went about their business merged into a hum of human voices from which no conversation was discernible.

1

A touch at her elbow brought Elizabeth's attention back to her companions.

"Do not meet their eyes," hissed her cousin, averting his own from the bustling scene in demonstration. "We shall be set upon by thieves!"

With a sigh Elizabeth relegated this last in a very long line of distressing non sequiturs to the back of her mind, all too aware that to actually listen to her cousin's blather would surely pave the path to madness.

At his cousin's marked disobedience the missionary merely tugged his black felt hat down further over his hair in a harrumph of displeasure while Elizabeth continued to lean out of their conveyance with undisguised interest in her surroundings.

"I assure you, Mr. Collins," offered Elizabeth's aunt on her behalf, "that we are quite unlikely to be accosted. Miss Elizabeth will be quite safe."

Elizabeth threw a grateful glance at her aunt before returning her attention to the market scene.

As they approached their destination the reflection of the sun on towering windows pierced white through the hanging goods and lanterns of the market street until the monolithic edifice filled Elizabeth's vision, plunging towards the sky in evident ignorance of its humble surroundings. Eschewing her cousin's proffered hand, Elizabeth stepped lightly out of the carriage without tearing her eyes from the monstrosity of the building before her. Upon presentation of their card to the opulently costumed native doorman, the group was admitted directly into a dining room that presented an unsettling resemblance to those of London. Like a bad satire,

2

the room was decorated in continental mimicry and buzzed with the familiar sound of English. The guests were dressed without exception in European styles, and the clothes that had set Elizabeth apart from the locals on the other side of the threshold gained her admittance to this exclusive party; the one requirement for entry to the Empire Club was to be white. Coiffed and groomed Arabs waited tables, weaving to and fro through the feathered and bespectacled diners. With a pang Elizabeth relinquished her yearnings for the scintillating Arabian market outside and resigned herself to an afternoon of conversation and tea that could have been found anywhere in Britain.

The ensuing hours did not disappoint on that score. In this scene, however, Elizabeth found herself to be the newest and most interesting topic of conversation amongst the ladies present.

"Miss Bennet," heralded a voice to her right, calling her attention to a well-dressed woman who had been introduced by her aunt as Mrs. Lennox. "Your aunt informs us that you are to cross the desert to Morocco with your uncle's caravan. We were quite unsure whether to believe it!"

"It is true," Elizabeth smiled, sipping her tea. "The caravan shall depart in but two days, and the desert crossing is expected to take thirty."

A collective gasp rose from the gathered Englishwomen. Mrs. Lennox once again took it upon herself to advocate for their horror.

"My dear," she admonished gravely. "Can it be *quite* safe?"

"To be quite safe," Elizabeth responded calmly, "one might as well have stayed at home in Hertfordshire."

"We are all aware of the dangers of the East, of course," assured

3

Mrs. Lennox, "else we should not have followed our husbands such a distance to live in this heathen land. But to travel alone—"

"Elizabeth will be protected by our most trusted guide," interjected Mrs. Gardiner, placing her hand on that of her niece. "My husband has made the journey many times under his care, and we trust him implicitly."

"But Madeline—with no chaperone!" protested the lady.

"Do you imply that you would prefer two females be subjected to the journey instead of one? If I can find such another lady who wishes to go as much as I do, I will take her with me forthwith," Elizabeth answered, momentarily silencing the objections.

"Our Elizabeth is a most unique and determined woman," Mrs. Gardiner explained, "and once her mind has settled on an idea, there is no crossing her."

"It seems not!" marveled Mrs. Lennox. "Very well, Miss Bennet. I do wish you Godspeed on your journey, though *I* should never undertake such a foolhardy venture."

"Then I consider it most fortunate that the opportunity has fallen before me instead of you, Mrs. Lennox," replied Elizabeth, smiling sweetly and excusing herself.

To Elizabeth, there was nothing scandalous about a lone female venturing into the desert. Indeed, she was too thrilled at the prospect to have considered any danger to be probable. At the scheme's first proposal Elizabeth had leapt at the chance to see the East, and at the tender age of twenty had become the first of her immediate family to venture outside the boundaries of the kingdom—indeed, past Europe itself and into this fantastic land whose ways and sensations could not have been further from those to which she was accustomed. On her first morning in the desert she had been awakened by the blazing sun on her face, the warbling of a Mohammedan at his devotions, and the pungent odor of native coffee. She had never known happiness so complete.

Her father had parted with her reluctantly, sending her across the continent and sea in the capable care of his sister-in-law, a young but sensible woman. Niece and aunt had long ago formed a close bond, and Elizabeth's father knew all too well how his daughter had envied her aunt the travels on which her husband's business took her. When Elizabeth had asked permission to go, he had known he could not refuse her a wish so dear to her heart. He named only one stipulation.

"Seek out my cousin Collins, my dear," her father had advised. "For though I have never seen him, I am told that he is a missionary in the very village to which you are traveling. Come to think of it, say nothing. I shall write to him informing him that you will be there, and I am certain he will appear at your doorstep. His exceedingly interesting letters appear with such regularity at mine, that I am positive that the merest chance would send him flying into your arms."

"Not literally I hope, Father," Elizabeth had laughed, overjoyed at the prospect of the journey ahead of her.

"If he should happen to trip and fall, do not go out of your way to avoid letting him grab you, Lizzy!" her mother had interrupted. "He is to inherit this estate, you know, when your father is dead, and may turn us out as soon as he pleases unless God grants us means to stay. It would be a very good match for both of you."

Her mother attempted a wink, both so exaggerated in its execution and vulgar in its connotation that Elizabeth could respond only with wide-eyed hor-

---

ror.

"Now, now, Lizzy," her father had reassured her. "You are under no such obligation. In fact, if his letters are any indication, I have great hopes of your finding him a most ridiculous specimen of manhood. Refuse him at your leisure."

"Do not speak so, Mr. Bennet!" cried his wife. "For you shall not be starving in the hedgerows with us after he inherits! Five daughters and an entailed estate is a trying situation indeed. Remember what I say, Lizzy!"

"Very well, Mamma," Elizabeth replied calmly. "In the event that this man, upon whom I have never laid eyes, should ask me for my hand while I am in Algiers, I promise faithfully to think on the advice of both my parents regarding the happy event."

Elizabeth was startled from her reverie by a familiar, hesitating touch at her elbow alerting her to her cousin's presence. With some amusement she acknowledged that her father's judgment of the man's character had been more than fulfilled, and the regular attentions paid by the gentleman had indeed become daily. To her dismay, however, the sheer absurdity of his character had prevented her deriving any pleasure from his company. Following the initial amusement attendant to her first exposure to the man, Elizabeth had quickly discovered that the unique mix of ingratiating humility and unflagging self-importance that comprised his personality wore out its welcome nearly instantly.

"Perhaps, my dearest cousin, some fresh air would revive your spirits?" he inquired with characteristic awkwardness.

Judging a moment away from the disapproving stares of the expatriate elite to be the lesser of two evils she accompanied him to the small, walled garden behind the Club. Once seated on a stone bench she breathed deep the warm air and leaned her head back to take in the bright dome of heaven.

"Cousin Elizabeth—" began her companion, trailing off.

"Yes?" Elizabeth prompted, mind elsewhere.

"My dear, dear cousin—"

Elizabeth knew at once that the moment she had dreaded was upon her. She had hoped to discourage her cousin's attentions blatantly enough to avoid this scene, but her cousin's perverse blindness to anything which did not suit his own wishes had evidently overthrown any doubts she might have been able to seed in a more sensible mind. Managing to drag her thoughts back from the depths of regret at her failure she registered that he had indeed continued to speak, and that she, as had become her habit, had succeeded in refusing to hear him.

"—lastly, it is my belief that every missionary should marry, and set the example of Holy Matrimony for the heathens to whom he brings the word of God. All these reasons, when coupled with your manifold charms and hardiness of body, to which these climes must indeed be less harmful, where a lady of more dainty proportions and constitution—well, as I was saying, your manifold charms—"

"Mr. Collins," Elizabeth interjected, pity taking precedence over manners on the point of interruption. "I am honored by your offer, but regret to say that I cannot accept it."

He was not cowed.

"Your modesty is merely one of your admirable qualities, cousin!" he gasped in deference. "If you mean to increase my love by suspense, rest assured—"

"I beg you, Mr. Collins, to drop your suit," pleaded Elizabeth, exasperation slipping into her voice despite her best efforts. "I have said that it is impossible, and I implore you to take my word."

"Dear cousin, I do not think I can have been mistaken on this point. The position of a missionary's wife and companion is nothing to be sniffed at," he insisted, changing strategies. He lowered his voice. "Furthermore, I think it very unlikely that another offer of marriage will ever be made to you. Your condition of relative poverty, the entailment of your father's estate upon me at the conclusion of my work here—"

"I am afraid, Sir, that I may listen no longer. We have been in the garden alone long enough, and I must beg to be excused."

"Cousin!" he cried in desperation. "You cannot intend to continue with this foolish journey! All sense of decorum prevents it! It would be the utmost folly—"

"I beg your pardon, Sir, but I do intend to undertake this journey. Nothing you say shall convince me otherwise, especially at this late date. Excuse me."

Ignoring her cousin's protestations at her precipitous departure, Elizabeth re-entered the club and pushed her way through the crowded hall to her aunt.

"Are you quite alright, Lizzy?" asked the older woman with concern at Elizabeth's distraught countenance. "Shall I fetch Mr. Collins, that we might start back to the hotel?"

"I beg you would not," said Elizabeth, a bit too quickly. Calming herself, she added: "If I might, I should prefer to return alone. It is barely a mile, and I will enjoy the walk."

With furrowed brow, her aunt studied Elizabeth's face. "Very well, Lizzy, but do not stray from the main road. I could never face your father if something were to happen to you."

"Thank you, Aunt," Elizabeth replied gratefully. She moved to the exit, a frantic breath held in until she emerged from the front of the building into the street. Only then did she release her sigh, and looked to the blindingly bright sky with unbidden tears misting her vision.

Her cousin's offer of marriage had indeed touched her, though not in the way he had hoped. His words were true enough—another offer of marriage might never be made to her. Elizabeth squeezed her eyes shut as she was unpleasantly reminded of a subject which had often occupied her mind.

As a young girl Elizabeth had vowed to marry only for the deepest love. In her twentieth year, however, fear was creeping in as she realized that love of any kind, even a passing fancy, had failed to come her way. Her father had raised her almost as a son, speaking to her of politics and about the books that interested him, and in return she had become tomboyish, apt to climb trees and run when unobserved. To her mother's vocally expressed dismay, Elizabeth had always stood apart from her four sisters in temper and interest. Still, she was the daughter of a gentleman and pretty enough, the striking aspects of her individual features merging into a harmonious whole that presented a pleasing if piquant aspect, and many local beaux had presented themselves with their hearts in their outstretched hands. None, however, had come so far as to propose, being promptly driven away by her unaffected reception. Elizabeth had realized with grief that her heart would not be easily touched, for she had wanted time and time again to feel stirrings of the love of which her sisters and friends had spoken. Never had a glimmer of romantic affection stirred her soul; at twenty she was untouched still, her body open to every physical sensation to be had in life, but her lips devoid of the memory of even one kiss.

Blinking back the tears that had sprung to her eyes, Elizabeth began to walk quickly in the direction of the hotel. Weaving through market stands and dusty byways with single-minded determination she approached a towering domed edifice, richly decorated with gilded orbs and bright painted designs which she had observed with interest on the way to the club. From within came bursts of laughter, shouting and the clack of tossed gaming chips.

As Elizabeth paused before the doors to regard the establishment with curiosity, the great entrance burst open and a cadre of striking young Arabs in robes of pure white poured out, cloaks floating about them entrancingly as they strode into the street. The sheiks were handsome and well-built, but their allure faded instantly when compared to the man who led them. He towered above the rest, tall and dark, his physical strength and grace of movement undeniable. His robes too were of purest white, but his were sashed about the trim waist with a swath of jet-black silk embroidered with silver thread, into which was thrust a revolver. He was laughing loudly with his men, white teeth gleaming from the most handsome face Elizabeth had ever beheld. Arab though he was, the planes of his face were perfectly aligned and the only concession made to his race by his perfect visage was the deep tan of a life spent in the desert.

At once Elizabeth was conscious of her own appearance, her bare head and thin English gown setting her immediately apart from the rabble in front of the club. The piercing gaze of the Sheik fell upon her at once, and Elizabeth felt the color rise to her face. He stopped the men behind him with a flick of his brown hand.

For what seemed an eternity Elizabeth and the Sheik regarded one another with open interest. The laughingly spoken gibes of the men behind him were incomprehensible to her, but she knew their meaning well enough. She felt compelled to break the lengthening impasse, though she knew it unlikely that the Arab would understand a word she said. Making up her mind to enter the beautiful building, she decided to use the elementary Arabic she had learned along the journey, comical though it would undoubtedly be.

"I am sorry," she said haltingly in the foreign tongue. "My way is in your way." She gestured toward the entrance from which he had emerged.

He continued to regard her for a moment more before he opened his mouth to speak, a heavy silence falling over the party in the echo of Elizabeth's hesitating declaration.

"I am most heartily disappointed that we have no common acquaintance to introduce us," he said at last, Cambridge English flowing from his lips with a clipped accent.

Elizabeth started, then flushed crimson once more.

"Elizabeth Bennet, Sir," she stammered, almost too stunned by his perfect diction to recall her own name.

"I am the Sheik Ahmed Ben Hassan," he replied with a long, low bow that accentuated the lean lines of his body. Elizabeth dropped a quick curtsey in acknowledgement.

His gaze met hers once more. "I am afraid that your interest in this establishment is in vain, Miss Bennet."

"And why is that, Sir?"

11

"This club is open only to Arabs," he stated, a slight raise of one eyebrow begging her to dispute his decree.

"You would bar me from this building?" she asked, meeting his challenge with the weapon of an archly sweet smile.

He seemed to be considering a reply when one of his subordinates offered, in French: "Shall we take her in as an offering to the marriage market? Many brides have been won today, but none so captivating as this one!" Laughter pealed at the remark, and Elizabeth took an unconscious step backward.

The Sheik finally tore his gaze from Elizabeth and glanced over his shoulder at his men, replying in kind: "She may captivate you, Yusef, but she is certainly not handsome enough to tempt me." Without another look in her direction he turned his head sharply and signaled to his men, who followed him in unison, robes billowing about their strong young bodies. The absence of his eyes upon her chilled Elizabeth as one feels the disappearance of the sun when it goes behind a cloud.

She stared for a time in disbelief at his retreating figure, a peal of laughter emerging a moment later as her mortification gave way to honest amusement at the sheer rudeness of the man. Elizabeth refused to allow his words of abuse to touch her heart. At the sound of her laugh the Sheik turned his head, meeting her eyes for another instant, expression inscrutable. With a frown he turned away once more, striding purposefully to his waiting horse and mounting it masterfully. As the sheiks disappeared into the crowd, Elizabeth struggled to conceal a smile. Turning on her heel she skipped lightly down the steps of the casino and returned to the street.

Chapter 2

Elizabeth's last day in Biskra was spent scrupulously avoiding her cousin, a feat more easily said than done. The obsequious parson remained unconvinced of her indifference to him, trying alternately by entreaty and threat to change her mind on the subject of their union. Recalling her father's advice, Elizabeth felt no compunction in ignoring his pleas. At last she managed to escape to her bed chamber, pleading a headache and begging her aunt to entertain her cousin as best she could.

"I am glad you have refused him, Lizzy," replied her aunt. "It was imprudent to be sure, with the estate entailed, but no one could blame you. I shall do the best I can to distract his attention this afternoon, but you must know that he was mentioned in our invitation to the Commandant's dinner tonight. I cannot refuse to include him now."

"Of course not," sighed Elizabeth, squeezing her aunt's hand. "Thank you for agreeing to entertain him today. I would not wish the task on anyone, but I fear I shall go mad if I must listen to his nonsense a minute more."

And so Elizabeth passed the chief of the day imprisoned in her room, longing all the while to be out in the city whose colors and sounds beckoned with exotic allure. Her only consolation lay in the thought that early the next morning she would ride out beyond the city walls and into the open desert, far from her cousin's unbearable prattle. With a wry smile she acknowledged that though she had once so longed to reach Biskra, she now longed even more to leave it. For the moment she was simply glad that after the following day she should not see her cousin again for years, if she could help it.

The Commandant's mansion, though modest by European standards, nonetheless offered the kind of luxury rarely seen in the region. The Commandant himself welcomed the pair with an air of confident hospitality, detached and polite, loath to truly engage with those of whom he would see little. They were guided to a large but comfortable parlor in which an eclectic group of guests were already conversing in twos and threes. It became apparent to Elizabeth that the Commandant's assemblies existed primarily to encourage the kind of cronyism that was also common in the West. Those with influence and those who wanted it rubbed elbows here far from the prying eyes of the nominal heads of state.

"Are you enjoying Biskra?" came a deep voice at her shoulder, accent clear and precise. Turning, Elizabeth was shocked to behold the visage of the handsome Sheik who had dismissed her so abruptly only a day before.

"Very much, Sir," she replied stumblingly, dropping a hasty curtsey. He nodded his head in acknowledgement of her deference.

"You are acquainted with the Commandant?" came a soft, feminine voice with a cultivated English accent. Elizabeth raised her eyes to meet those of a strikingly beautiful woman who had just looped her arm through the Sheik's. Her skin was lighter than his, and her glossy black hair was piled atop a nobly-held head. About her throat a scattered constellation of jewels sparkled in the lamplight.

"Not at all," Elizabeth admitted readily. "My aunt, Mrs. Gardiner, was able to secure us an invitation on her former acquaintance."

"Gardiner..." searched the lady thoughtfully. "Her husband must be a diplomat...?"

"Quite the contrary," replied Elizabeth. "My uncle trades in the import of textiles through his business in London."

A shadow passed over the woman's face, and she cast an unacknowledged glance at the Sheik beside her. "I had no idea the Commandant associated with such a type. He does not look like a businessman, however, I daresay."

15

Elizabeth followed the lady's gaze to Mr. Collins, upon whom her disdainful frown was fixed.

"You are mistaken," she corrected. "That man is my cousin Mr. Collins. He is engaged in missionary work in Biskra at present."

"A missionary!" cried the woman, finely sculpted brows raised in disgust. "There are more underfoot than rats at a poorhouse. I intend no offense to your cousin, but I should bid them as good of riddance."

The woman laughed lightly, a melodic sound that pleased the ear but carried no feeling. She smiled conspiratorially at the Sheik, whose gaze was directly levelly to the distance.

"Come now, Ahmed," she prodded. "I know you despise the proselytizers as much as I do!"

Without moving the Sheik replied, "They would as well have stayed in England."

"You do not believe, then," interjected Elizabeth, "in the benefits of cultural exchange?"

The Sheik's dark gaze found hers once more. "The exchange moves in but one direction, where religion is concerned," he scowled. "And you? You are here to convert the heathens as well?"

"I am here to learn," Elizabeth said plainly. She was met by silence. "I judge that you have spent some years in England yourself, Sir. Was the experience not beneficial? Was your understanding not improved by the knowledge of a culture other than your own?"

"No," he said darkly. "It was not."

"You must understand, Miss – " The fine lady paused, realizing too late that she had not been introduced.

"Bennet," said the Sheik and Elizabeth in unison. Elizabeth

flushed brightly at the realization that the Sheik had bothered to recall her name. The Sheik merely set his jaw and stared at the far wall.

"*Bennet*," continued the lady, with a concerned glance at the Sheik, "that dear Ahmed cannot abide the English, though he did indeed study there. Found them *barbarians*, I believe was the word. I fear he will be unlikely to approve of your little pleasure trip into our land, however well-intentioned."

Faced by the implacable countenances of the imposing duo, Elizabeth ceded temporary defeat. With a curt bow she turned and located her aunt, joining her with a bright smile for the uniformed man with whom she was conversing. A few moments later she succeeded in charming a peal of laughter from the French officer, and wisely refrained from stealing a glance of triumph at the Sheik and his partner.

Elizabeth managed to think no more of the dark, handsome Sheik until dinner was served and she found herself seated directly across from him and his finely dressed companion. The lady made a show of leaning to whisper in the Sheik's ear at any available opportunity, but received only monosyllables from him for her pains.

To Elizabeth's dismay, Collins had spent enough time in the company to be at his ease, and his voice began to carry up and down the table. More than once Elizabeth found herself unable to meet the burning gaze of the Sheik as plentiful inanities escaped her cousin's lips. The fine lady was equally unimpressed, smirking silently behind her hand.

Before long Mr. Collins had engaged the unfortunate Commandant in conversation, expounding on the virtues of the ladies at the table.

"Never have I seen such fine manners!" cried Collins, completely unaware of any irony he might be producing. "Whether in London, Kent or indeed Biskra, there are so many fine examples of good breeding and true accomplishment in the elegant female! Each in her own way a jewel! Far above others of her sex who think themselves to be more important than they are."

Elizabeth could not help but feel that he was referring to her.

"I do not know half a dozen women that I would consider truly well-bred," said the Sheik, opening his mouth for the first time to the general company.

Collins was temporarily stymied.

"And what, may I ask, Mr. Collins, is your idea of good breeding?" asked the Sheik's companion innocently.

"The talents of the sex are limitless, Madam," Collins said gravely, directing a pointed stare at his cousin. "Many are artistes at the pianoforte or harp, others sing, cover screens and I know not what."

"Astounding," responded the lady in tones of utmost seriousness. The Sheik's glare deepened, and he focused his gaze on the glint of candlelight captured in the stem of his wine glass as he pinched it between his fingers.

"And verses!" continued Collins, oblivious. "Lovely bits of verses may be attributed to a lady's hand as well!"

"But there falls the end of her attractions," added Elizabeth quickly, striving by any action to delay her cousin's effusions. "The most accomplished of ladies should never endeavor to add the title of poetess to her list of skills, I venture, for it can only end badly. Indeed, I wonder who first discovered the efficacy of poetry in driving away love?"

"I had been used to consider poetry the food of love," the Sheik said suddenly, commanding all eyes.

Elizabeth's sparkled as she replied: "Of a fine, stout, healthy love it may. But if it be only a slight, thin sort of inclination, I am convinced that one good sonnet will starve it entirely away."

The Sheik eyed Elizabeth darkly, brow furrowed as he considered her arch invitation to verbal battle.

"All of these talents, of course!" interjected the Sheik's companion, unsettled by the developing *tete-a-tete*, "But these cannot stand alone. A truly accomplished woman must possess a certain nobility of bearing, a modulation of voice, an elegance at all times in her manner of walking, and of speaking." The emphatic mode of the lady's declaration made less clear her point and more her belief in her own accomplishments, and Elizabeth was surprised to detect a pinkening of the Sheik's countenance in mortification at his companion's boldness. Nevertheless, Collins was quite convinced.

"Indeed!" he cried.

"But to all of this," added the Sheik solemnly, silencing the debate with the finality of his tone, "must be added something more, in the improvement of her understanding by extensive travel."

Elizabeth raised her eyebrows, and decided to contribute. "I am no longer surprised at your knowing only *six* accomplished women, Sir," she declared. "I rather wonder at your knowing any."

The Sheik started, and directed his piercing gaze at Elizabeth. His reaction to being contradicted revealed his utter lack of familiarity with the experience.

"You are too severe upon your own sex, Miss Bennet!" cried

the lady. "Perhaps you have not had the advantage of moving in society enough. I assure you that there are many *very* accomplished women among our acquaintance." With this she tried to recapture the Sheik's gaze, to little avail.

"I speak as I find," said Elizabeth steadily.

The Sheik broke his stare at her and lowered his eyes, hiding his mouth briefly behind his clenched fist. Elizabeth had rarely encountered such blatant hostility, but knew she was equal to it.

"Speaking of travel," attempted the lady, breaking a lengthy silence, "have I ever regaled you, Commandant, with a retelling of my travels into India? The experience was quite thrilling!"

With a dismissive glance at Elizabeth, she launched into a veritable soliloquy on the subject, releasing her domination over the conversation only with the eventual dissolution of the party.

Following dinner, a short period of entertainment was proposed, and Elizabeth was prevailed upon to play at the pianoforte. At the conclusion of her simple song, she raised her eyes to the politely applauding company and was disconcerted to meet the scrutiny of the Sheik. His gaze in her direction was quite profound, and when placed beside the unimpressed countenance of his companion, seemed certain to be the result of his continued disapproval of her. Releasing the breath she held, Elizabeth rose and managed a smile as she ceded the instrument. Her place was quickly taken by the Sheik's companion, who displayed her prowess with a brisk rendition of one of Mozart's more complicated works.

As the lady began to play the Sheik moved to stand, eyes still clapped on Elizabeth's blushing face. In the same instant that Elizabeth realized he meant to move towards her, she was accosted by her cousin, who whispered to her in tones audible by their subject: "I have just learnt that the gentleman you see there is the sheik Ahmed Ben Hassan, ruler of vast expanses of territory and a man of boundless influence in this part of the world. I must make myself known to him."

"Sir!" cried Elizabeth in distress. "You have not been introduced. He will consider it an impertinence!"

"I find, dear cousin, that the social mores which govern society in England are transcended even in that land by the span of influence of a clergyman, and indeed in this heathen country such rules cannot hold. He may be able to assist my cause in reaching the peoples of the desert. I am quite determined," stated Mr. Collins, already moving toward the Sheik.

The taller man, observing the intercourse between Elizabeth and her cousin, was paused uncomfortably in evident indecision. His discomfort, however, was increased incalculably by the assault upon his senses rendered by the approach of Mr. Collins. Elizabeth could not help but overhear the discourse between them, one-sided though it was, and flushed brightly with humiliation at her cousin's blunders. The Sheik knew not which way to look as Collins tried one subject and then another to gain his ear.

"You are a great connoisseur of music, I think, your excellence?" attempted Collins, seeing the Sheik's gaze alight on his companion at the pianoforte.

"Quite the contrary," replied the Sheik shortly.

"Your lady friend plays exquisitely! You have, no doubt, had many occasions to appreciate her talents."

"Madame de Veilleux has had the benefit of the masters," an-

21

swered the Sheik. "I rarely hear her, however, as I own no instrument."

"I fear my charming cousin's performance can have been be nothing to hers, of course," conceded Collins, prompting Elizabeth to avert her eyes to hide her mortification. "I have high hopes, nevertheless, that after the day on which she honors me with her hand she shall have ample opportunity of honing her craft on the instrument of my noble patroness, Lady Catherine de Bourgh. I should say *one* of her Ladyship's instruments, for she—"

The Sheik's eyes turned in disbelief to Collins, an unmistakable expression of shock forming on his countenance. Elizabeth overheard her cousin's remark as well, and found herself desiring nothing more than to fall through the floor and disappear. As that was unlikely to happen, she instead turned her mind to a method, any method, of halting his discourse with the Sheik. With purposeful strides she crossed the room and endeavored to engage his attentions elsewhere.

"Mr. Collins," she cried. "You must come away. The...er...officers you see there are quite at odds on a question of profound theological importance."

Collins was drawn away at once. "My dear cousin," he exclaimed, "why did you not consult me sooner? Excuse me, your excellence, for my humble powers are required to assist in this dispute."

As Collins retreated in search of the elusive debaters, Elizabeth found herself suddenly thrust into the company of the Sheik, from whom she felt she could not disengage herself without giving offense. As she searched her mind for an excuse, she was surprised to see him move closer to her and lean his head near hers.

"Miss Bennet," he said softly, "may I have the privilege of speaking to you privately?"

Elizabeth's shock at the request was overshadowed by a discordant clash of notes that suddenly emitted from the pianoforte. Madame de Veilleux, eyes clapped on the figures of Elizabeth and the Sheik, stumbled badly in her piece before recovering her countenance and playing on. Elizabeth took the opportunity of changing the subject, uncertain of what might have come of her acceptance of the Sheik's request.

"Mozart's work is lovely, but far beyond my talents. Madame de Veilleux is bold in her choice."

The Sheik frowned darkly at Elizabeth before replying: "Mozart is too complex for my taste."

"Perhaps you and the Emperor Joseph are in agreement then," ventured Elizabeth. "Though I doubt Madame de Veilleux would appreciate his thoughts on the subject at this particular moment, and might interpret them rather as criticism of her performance."

"What had the Emperor to say?" asked the Sheik.

" 'Too many notes,'" replied Elizabeth with a mischievous smile.

Excusing herself, she moved across the room to rejoin her aunt. Mrs. Gardiner was speaking with a dark man in the uniform of a French officer whose easy manners and expression endeared him immediately to Elizabeth.

"Elizabeth," said her aunt enthusiastically. "You have not yet met your guide. This is Ibraheim Omair."

The man made a low bow over Elizabeth's proffered hand, bright eyes meeting hers with open friendliness. His grasp on her hand tightened unexpectedly, however, as his gaze flitted over her shoulder. Turning, Elizabeth beheld the towering form of the Sheik, countenance overcome with a flush of anger as his eyes met Omair's. Omair himself paled, dropping Elizabeth's hand hastily and executing a formal bow in the direction of the Sheik. Before he raised his head the Sheik had turned away, quickly making his way to the pianoforte and rousing Madame de Veilleux from her seat. He whispered a few words in her ear before abandoning her and heading toward the Commandant.

These motions were beheld with apparent apprehension by Ibraheim Omair, though a moment later he regained his former charm.

"I beg your pardon, Miss Bennet," he said with regret. "I must be going. I look forward to seeing you tomorrow morning, and to the journey ahead."

Elizabeth and her aunt watched with confusion as the young man effected a hasty retreat, his figure disappearing almost before Elizabeth could open her mouth to acknowledge his departure. Unable to account for the awkwardness of the two men on beholding one another, Elizabeth was some moments in cogitation over what had occurred. Her curiosity was not to be sated, however, for though the Sheik's agitated stare often fell upon her form throughout the course of the evening, he did not venture to speak to her again.

- The Sheik of Araby -

That evening Elizabeth finished packing her clothes and supplies for the long journey that would begin at dawn the next morning. Brushing out her mass of dark curls, Elizabeth thought back on the odd tone that had marked her encounters with the mysterious Sheik. She knew she irked him, though she was at a loss to say why his ire had been so instantly raised against her. The mere fact of her nationality did not seem enough, especially since he had sat next to a dark lady with an English accent the entire evening. Resolving to forget his arrogant presumption forever and turn her attention to the future, Elizabeth pushed all thoughts of the Sheik out of her mind.

The city was now largely silent, and most people were in bed. Elizabeth crossed to the balcony once more, inhaling deeply the Eastern air and leaning over the banister into the night. A voice drifted to her ears from far away, singing, strangely enough, in English. It was a low baritone, caressing a lilting Eastern melody with great strength and joy. The words came to her ears and arrested her while they lasted.

> *Pale hands I loved,*
> *Beside the Shalimar.*
> *Where are you now?*
> *Who lies beneath your spell?*
>
> *Whom do you lead on*
> *Rapture's roadway far,*
> *Before you agonize*
> *Them in farewell?*

Elizabeth strained to hear the final notes as they died on the breeze, heart beating quickly as she closed her eyes and listened to the plaintive tune. Who could love so, that he sang to the sky in his ardor? She wondered who the creature could be, who inspired such beautiful and melancholy words. A vision arose of an Arabian princess, veiled and gowned in bright silk and gold, eyes rimmed in darkest kohl and delicate bare feet dipping into a God-sent oasis. With a smile at her own bare toes peeking from beneath her nightgown and chilled by the tile floor beneath her feet, Elizabeth retreated to the welcoming softness of her bed. Still smiling, she leaned across the side table and extinguished the flame of her lamp.

Chapter 3

The midmorning sun beat down hotter than Elizabeth had ever felt it as her journey into the desert began in earnest. She had that morning bid a cheerful farewell to her cousin and heartfelt adieu to her aunt, and started with the caravan in high spirits. She had at first balked at the necessity for long sleeves and gloves in the stifling heat, but had quickly realized that they and her wide-brimmed, heavily veiled helmet were all that kept her pale skin from being scorched by the sun's merciless rays.

Elizabeth had never considered herself a horsewoman, but riding in a canopied box atop a camel was more insult than luxury in her mind. She had been given, therefore, a gentle mount named Lujine who bore her evenly across the dunes. She also found herself wearing breeches and tall boots, as riding sidesaddle for any such length of time was a sheer impossibility. And so, thus garbed, Elizabeth released herself over to the exotic. Indeed, in this place no social normative could hold. She felt completely free for the first time in her memory, her mind hearkening back to the sensation of running down the path from Oakham Mount as fast as her legs could take her. In Hertfordshire, however, propriety and restraint had always awaited her at the end of her headlong run. With joy rising uncontrollably in her bosom she raised her veiled head to the sky and basked in the warmth of the blazing sun on her face. A sensation of great anticipation took hold of her, as though her life were about to begin.

Ibraheim Omair had taken up a position just behind her. Their caravan moved slowly but steadily away from Biskra and the safety it provided. Ahead of them Elizabeth could see nothing but sand, the heat radiating off of the dunes in undulating waves. No tree, no shrub interrupted the unending expanse. As far as the eye could see, the pale blue sky met the horizon in a shifting sea of heat.

Some time in the mid-afternoon an oasis at last shimmered in the distance. With a little cry of surprise, Elizabeth caught Omair's attention and pointed it out to him. A knowing smile was returned for her troubles. With a slight flush of embarrassment Elizabeth realized that the oasis had been their destination. It had seemed impossible to her that the desert could be navigable, its notable spots recorded or known. But, as did the sea to which she had compared it, the desert shared the secrets of its vastness with the men who gave their lives to travel upon it.

The shade of the date palms was heavenly, and Elizabeth lounged happily for some time as the men watered their beasts. She unpinned the broad hat from her dark curls and fanned her face with it, reveling in the chill of the breeze against her damp skin. A meal of bread and olives was procured for her, and she ate gratefully. Never before had she known such a day. Too soon, however, the shadow of the guide fell across her.

"Is everything to your liking, Madame?" he asked amiably.

"Yes," smiled Elizabeth. "I thank you."

"It is a rare pleasure to be permitted the company of so lovely a lady," added Omair, a disarming smile crossing his features. His figure was fine, tall body swathed in a burnous of dark red cloth. Hanging against his side a shining sword glimmered. "May I sit?"

"Of course," replied Elizabeth. "Is it not time we continued, however?"

"We will wait until the sun falls lower," he replied, seating himself next to her in the shade of the palm. They sat some moments in silence, regarding the endless expanse of desert before them.

"I must apologize for my rudeness last night," he said at last. "I have been wondering all day how to account for it, when next I spoke to you. Are you much acquainted with Ahmed Ben Hassan?"

Elizabeth, surprised at his confession, managed to reply: "Only a little. We met but two days ago."

"You think him an honorable man?"

"I could not tell you," replied Elizabeth honestly. "His manners have impressed me as abrupt, and I can safely say that I do not care to know him any better."

Omair allowed a slight smile at her words, eyes gazing thoughtfully into the distance. "I am surprised to hear you say it," he said.

29

"There are very few besides myself who share the opinion, I am certain."

Elizabeth was struck once again by the openness of his countenance, and could not help but admit to herself that though his skin was a dark shade of brown, she thought him very handsome.

"Would it surprise you to know that Ahmed and I were raised together, in the same camp?"

Elizabeth's expression did indeed betray her surprise, prompting the guide to continue.

"Indeed," he went on, "for you no doubt noticed the cold manner of our greeting last night. I had determined to tell you all, for the truth is what you deserve, but I should not have wished to give you pain. It is a very great wrong that was done me by Ahmed Ben Hassan."

Elizabeth's color rose, animation increasing as she said, "You can have no fear of alarming me on his account, for I have only reason to think him very disagreeable."

"I loved my father more than my life," Omair began. "He was second-in-command to Ahmed's father, and together they ruled a vast territory until my own father's early death. His father loved me as a son, and Ahmed and I played together from childhood. He was of a jealous nature, however, and for every caress his father bestowed on me I would later receive a blow from the son. He could not bear to think that his father loved me better."

Elizabeth's concern was apparent as she regarded the earnest countenance of the storyteller in rapt attention.

"Despite that, I could never hold against him the actions of our boyhood. Once we were grown, however, his temper turned even darker, and could be called resentful. He has often boasted that his good opinion, once lost, is lost forever. I was unfortunate enough to lose his esteem too early, and the cost would be the loss of the woman I loved."

Elizabeth gasped. "What can you mean?"

"Ahmed's father wished him to have the best education possible, sending him to England for years while I managed the day-to-day affairs of the tribe in his place. During Ahmed's absence his father sickened. On the old Sheik's death Ahmed returned to our tribe, casting me aside with impunity despite his father's dying wish that I remain beside the new sheik, as my father had served the old. I would not have cared, for myself, but in banishing me from my home and stripping me of my possessions, he also separated me forever from the dearest object of my heart. She was only a servant girl, but we loved each other. As far as I know she lives there still, serving him. I cannot bear to think of how he may have dishonored her, for the extent of his spite for me never knew bounds."

"I cannot believe it!" cried Elizabeth, tears threatening.

Omair glanced to her, seeming to awake from a reverie of memories. On perceiving her distress he immediately moderated his voice.

"I have shocked you," he said penitently. "There is no place for tears on your beautiful face. You see that I live, and that my life is good. Though I am no Sheik, I am happy. Though I am exiled from my tribe, I have found honest employment."

Drying her tears, Elizabeth attempted a smile. "You bear your ill treatment as few could," she said at last.

"No joy can come from mourning what cannot be changed,"

he replied with a sad smile.

Heart softened, Elizabeth regarded Omair in steady concentration. It seemed impossible that one so good could have been used so infamously. Before she could make sense of the emotions that tumbled through her at the sight of him, the guide stood and offered her his hand.

"It is time to leave, Madame," he said gently, eyes meeting hers in silent entreaty.

Reluctantly Elizabeth replaced her helmet and did as he asked. Within minutes the caravan was again moving steadily across the desert.

The sun was low in the western sky when Elizabeth saw one of the men of the caravan ride up to Omair. They exchanged a few words and Omair looked, frowning, to the horizon. Just then there appeared the faintest shape in the undulating dusk, a smudge of black against the desert, miles away. Elizabeth watched the low shape as it grew until she could discern its individual parts – men on horseback, galloping at unbelievable speed directly toward them. Unsure how to act, she looked to Omair. He was directing his men, gesturing fiercely, and Elizabeth was forgotten in the commotion that ensued. The horses and camels scattered as the beasts felt the rumble of hooves in the ground beneath their feet. Men reined in their rearing horses. The horde was close now– Arabs on horse-back, rifles clutched in their hands as they galloped ever closer. A shot rang out.

Chaos erupted as Ibraheim Omair toppled from his horse, landing with a heavy thud at its feet.

"Ibraheim!" screamed Elizabeth in horror, eyes fixed on his writhing form.

The men of the caravan, with shouts of surprise, leveled their rifles and fired back at the attackers. Driven wild by the cacophony of rifle fire Elizabeth's horse bolted away from the caravan, heedless to any attempt her rider made to control her. Powerless, Elizabeth clutched the reins as tightly as she could and ducked her head as bullets whistled past her ears.

The sounds of shouting and ringing shots faded as the horse scrambled away from the scene, and at some point in the uncontrolled gallop Elizabeth's broad-brimmed helmet tore from her head and fell against her back, hairpins clinging to her curls. Tears and sand stung at her eyes as she closed them tight and prayed to escape the situation into which she had been suddenly thrust. Surely they were not yet too far from Biskra. A night's journey, perhaps. She might live to tell this tale.

The deafening ping of a shot rang by her ear, closer than the sounds of chaos she was leaving behind. Elizabeth wrenched her head around to see that a lone stallion was gaining on her, the man astride leaning low in the saddle. With a sickening sensation in her stomach Elizabeth realized that she had no chance. Her horse could never outrun the magnificent Arabian he rode. Still, she urged her mount onward. Death awaited when he caught up with her, she was certain. Perhaps it was only delaying the inevitable, but Elizabeth's powerful will to live surged up and drove her forward.

A whistle sounded, and her horse pricked up her ears. Suddenly the beast wheeled to a stop, sides heaving.

"Go!" Elizabeth cried, pulling at the reins. "Damn you, run!"

But it was too late. The Arab was upon her.

The great Arabian slowed as it approached, and the last thing Elizabeth saw before closing her eyes in terror was the gleam of white teeth as the rider smiled.

The blow she had been expecting, either of bullet or sword, never came. She was caught roughly about the waist and her feet were jerked from the stirrups. Cloth enfolded her, blocking her view and binding her limbs. She struggled, hard, but the arm that held her tightened like an iron band. The Arab was holding her, tightly, before him on his horse. Wind whipped her curls into her eyes and mouth, and she struggled once more to free herself. The arm tightened until she could no longer breathe, her rib cage crushed in the harsh embrace. Darkness overcame her vision and she gave herself gratefully to the void.

Chapter 4

Elizabeth's mind roused itself before her eyes opened, fingers grasping blindly at the surface on which she lay. A momentary surety that she would feel the soft, worn surface of the quilt on her bed at home was quickly dashed. Brocade rasped beneath her fingers. Her head rested on silk. Her nostrils were assaulted by the thick scent of incense and native coffee. Her eyes opened painfully, focus coming only with great concentration.

The room in which she found herself was not really a room at all, but was just as large. Its draped walls revealed it to be part of a huge tent, sumptuously hung with tapestries and Eastern art works. She lay upon a low, soft bed, body filthy with sand and wearing her riding clothes.

A small sound turned her head, and she faced a thin brown girl in a clean but unadorned robe. The girl's large eyes widened as she saw that Elizabeth had awoken. She turned to leave.

"Wait!" Elizabeth cried. Her throat was sore. A tentative movement showed her, painfully, that her entire body was sore from her unchecked struggle with the Arab. "Where am I?"

"You are in the camp of the great Sheik," the brown girl replied in hesitating French. Elizabeth attempted to answer in kind, but the language was difficult for both.

"Where is the Sheik?" she asked.

"He awaits. I am to bathe you."

"You shall do no such thing," Elizabeth blurted out in English, startling the girl back into silence. With immense effort Elizabeth struggled to her feet.

From the opposite end of the room came the soft noise of the heavy curtain being drawn back. Elizabeth turned in time to see a tall, imposing figure step through the opening. Clad in a white burnous with a black sash, his handsome face somber, Elizabeth recognized at once the dark, stoic Sheik she had met in Biskra. He had discarded his outer robes and removed his keffiyeh, exposing for the first time his close-cropped black locks and high brow. With the slightest lift of his chin he banished the girl, who disappeared instantly behind another curtain.

"You are awake," the Sheik stated.

"As you see," Elizabeth replied, tension building in her chest as he advanced towards her, slowly.

"The girl Zilah will serve you here," he continued, casually, as though she had been an invited guest. "She will provide you with anything you need."

Disbelief was foremost in Elizabeth's reeling mind as she realized for what purpose she had been brought.

"Someone in Biskra will know I am missing," she said boldly, attempting vainly to stave him off with a glare. "My plans—"

"Your aunt saw you off on a month's journey into the desert. Your uncle does not expect you until that time. No one shall miss you, until it is much too late."

Elizabeth's eyes widened in shock. "How do you know my schedule?"

"Everything can be gained, for a price." Regaining her composure, Elizabeth raised her chin and tried to hide her fear in an icy stare. "There you are wrong."

The Sheik chose to ignore her defiance, instead flashing his white teeth briefly in an ironic smile.

"Why have you brought me here?" Elizabeth asked, dreading his answer. She knew a man like this would capture a lone woman for only one purpose.

He raised an eyebrow as if in question before answering, "Are you not woman enough to know?"

A crimson blush spread up Elizabeth's neck and into her cheeks, flushing them bright red. She took an instinctive step backward, only to stumble against a low object on the floor. Glancing back, she realized with a sinking feeling that she had stumbled against her own trunk, open, her clothes unpacked and in order. Her toiletries were arranged on a fine vanity inlaid with rich wood.

"I will not yield to you," Elizabeth said with as much conviction as she could muster.

"Your ungratefulness does you no credit, Miss Bennet," he said sternly.

"Ungratefulness!" she cried. "Am I to be grateful?"

"Others were only too happy to be chosen. Do you know what Zilah would give for my notice? Or any daughter of Biskra? You are English, but you cannot fail to welcome what other women would happily die for."

Elizabeth scoffed. "You are correct; I am English. As such, I am not to be picked up and discarded according to your Eastern fancy."

"I have offered you the luxury and protection of my tent. These are no small favors, in the desert. Without them, you will die."

"Heavy misfortune, indeed!" Elizabeth cried sarcastically. The Sheik's countenance turned dark.

"And this is all the reply I am to expect?" he asked, eyes alight with anger.

"One might wonder, with what little regard for my happiness and honor I am thus abducted? No gentleman of the West would dream to do such a thing. I suppose it is your birthright!"

"More than you know," he growled, the color rising in his handsome face. Elizabeth knew she was provoking him, but could find no reason to stop. He could kill her, for all she cared.

"Since the first moment I saw you, you impressed me with your selfish disdain for the feelings of others. I had not conversed with you a minute before knowing that I would rather die than sleep next to you."

The Sheik's eyes flashed bright.

"You would prefer the bed of Collins, I suppose," he seethed.

"I should have known that your eagerness to learn was pretense alone, and that like most of your race you despise a man whose skin is darker than your own."

Elizabeth's mind seized at his first words, and her mouth opened in disbelief. "Of Collins!" she cried in disbelief. "What involvement has he with what you have done?"

"He made it quite clear that you had formed an understanding. I see that I was incorrect after all regarding your feelings towards him."

"Correct or not, you presumed all," replied Elizabeth, recovering slightly. "I can see that my conclusions regarding your character were well justified. You care nothing for those around you, and supersede their wishes with your own. And yet it is not merely on my own observation that my dislike is founded," she continued. "Your character was decided when I heard Ibraheim Omair's recital of your dealings with him."

The Sheik's color rose and he took a step back, her words striking him with the force of a blow.

"You take an eager interest in his concerns, it seems," he said coldly.

"Who that knows what his misfortunes have been, could help feeling an interest in him?"

"His misfortunes!" repeated the Sheik contemptuously, "Yes, his misfortunes have been great indeed!"

"And of your infliction," cried Elizabeth. "Can you begin to defend your infamous behavior on that score?"

"My faults, according to this calculation, are heavy indeed," replied the Sheik, countenance controlled only by great effort. "You have made your feelings on the subject quite clear. I have only to be ashamed of what my own have been."

Elizabeth seized at his contrition. "If you are in possession of any humanity at all, Sir, then I beg of you to redeem yourself and release me from this imprisonment."

His expression closed as he set his jaw and stared past her shoulder.

"I cannot."

The agony of her situation overcame Elizabeth's resolve and her eyes began to cloud with tears. The Sheik averted his eyes, calmly ignoring her plight.

"You will sleep alone tonight," he said evenly, turning his back and striding out of the chamber.

Elizabeth sat down heavily on the luxurious bed. Anger was quickly overcome by despair as she realized the futility of her situation. Her fight against the Sheik on the back of the great Arabian horse had ended in his crushing the breath out of her with one arm. She had no hope of escape. He would have his way with her; there was no question of that. It was clear that he considered her his property, his mistress. At the first introduction of the word into her mind, Elizabeth's every sensibility rebelled. Frantically she raised her eyes, searching for an implement for her last, desperate act.

There was nothing. He was too clever for her. She could not even take the coward's way out, and she cursed him for stopping her. With a great, gasping sob Elizabeth clung to the fine bed-clothes and struggled for air. She cursed the name of the Sheik, its foreign syllables biting on her tongue. She cursed the day her uncle had first traveled to the East, bringing back tales of exotic scenes and peoples. She cursed the guide for his failure to protect her. More than anything, she cursed herself for foolish pride. She had thought she was invincible. She was being forced, painfully, to learn that she was not.

At the gentle touch of the silk sheets against her bruised flesh, her mind fought back again at what had been done to her. Tears flooded to her eyes, scorching in hot trails down her cheeks as she gripped the silk in blindly grasping fists. She wept, crying out to the empty room in supplication. She begged escape from this Arab camp. She begged release from the terror she faced. Her sobs subsided at last, resolving into a stupor of exhaustion and grief. As hours passed following the Sheik's departure, Elizabeth resigned herself to at least scrubbing the sand and grit from her abused body. The girl, Zilah, replied at once to her hesitant call and prepared the finest bath she had ever known. The water was warmed to perfection, and oils and spices had been added to the water. Elizabeth's senses were overcome, and her body relaxed despite itself. No sooner had she stepped out of the water and into a silk robe than the overwhelming urge to crawl back into the brocaded bed claimed her and she fell into a deep and dreamless slumber.

When she awoke, grey light was making its way into the ventilation slits of the heavy canvas tent. A broad slash fell across her pillow, and she turned her head in irritation to banish its harsh reminder that she must awake and face the day.

Elizabeth rolled over drowsily. The scent of coffee pervaded the room, brightening Elizabeth's senses as she shook off the weight of sleep. Perceiving that she was alone, Elizabeth dressed quickly and emerged from the bed chamber, senses alert to all around her. Crossing the main room she ventured to push aside the heavy outer curtain. The camp was desolate, no movement discernible from any of the neighboring tents. A moment later a piercing scream split the air and stood Elizabeth's hair instantly on end.

Insensible to any danger, Elizabeth began to run in the direction of the sound. On approaching the source, the murmur of a crowd was readily audible. Soon she rounded a large tent and beheld the wide encircling fences of a corral and the press of a large crowd around it. In the center a lithe young colt pranced skittishly, tossing its head with crazed, angry motions. Beside the colt stood the Sheik, eyes narrowed as he approached the maddened animal. In the instant that the colt began to buck away from his extended hand he clamped the bridle in his fist and swung himself lightly onto the horse's back. Enraged, the horse flung itself upward in an effort to unseat him, flailing wildly and cutting the bit deep into its blood-smeared muzzle. The Sheik would not be thrown. He clung with relentless determination to the back of the frenzied mount, pitting his own strength against the horse's and his will against that of the unbroken animal. Elizabeth had witnessed the breaking of a colt before, but never had she beheld an animal fighting so desperately against control. The man fought the horse and the horse the man, blood and perspiration flying from both to dampen the sandy ground.

Elizabeth wanted to close her eyes, to look away from the unbearably painful spectacle before her. As she watched the wild creature struggle beneath the masterful grip of the Sheik she recalled her own fight against him, felt an echo of his arm grasping her to his body, remembered the desperation of her struggle and its ultimate futility.

"Madame?" came a voice from behind her. Glancing behind her, Elizabeth recognized the serving girl whom she had met the night before.

"It is horrible," cried Elizabeth, shaken. "He will murder the poor beast."

"The horse has killed a man this morning," replied Zilah softly, "savaged him, as you say. Yusef was thrown next. No one else will attempt it."

Minutes stretched on as the Sheik clung to the back of the bucking beast, resisting every attempt to shake him off. At last the colt's muscles began to slacken, eyes rolling back in a final bid for freedom. The Sheik clenched his jaw and renewed his iron grip on the animal, forcing the fight to the finish. With one last heaving sigh the horse conceded, limbs falling pliably into the Sheik's control.

As the beast fell silent the Sheik slowly dismounted, walking with some pain to the edge of the corral. Tribesmen viewed him with awe as he left the creature foaming and beaten at the center of the sandy enclosure. At the Sheik's weary signal another man dashed up to the colt and quickly grasped its bridle.

"Come, Madame," said Zilah. "Allow me to plait your hair."

With a frown Elizabeth let herself be gently pulled away from the corral, tearing her eyes from the towering form of the Sheik with some difficulty. Back in the tent she sat silently, replaying the desperate struggle she had just witnessed and wondering at the stark realities of life in the desert.

A sound outside her chamber alerted Elizabeth to the Sheik's presence and she stood automatically, heedless of Zilah's protests. A moment later her hair was finished and she walked quickly into the main room of the tent.

"Good morning, Miss Bennet."

Elizabeth could scarcely believe her eyes. The Sheik, who had only half an hour before thrown his body and soul into a bloody conflict was now impeccably groomed and disconcertingly calm. He halted her by rising to his feet, his full height so impressive that Elizabeth was fixed to the spot.

"You must be famished," observed the Sheik, eyeing her critically. His dark eyes were unnervingly penetrating as he surveyed her appearance. "I shall have Gaston bring your breakfast."

The Sheik's gaze finally left Elizabeth's body and he snapped his fingers. Instantly a small Frenchman appeared at the door of the tent.

"Madame's breakfast," the Sheik said curtly in French. The servant made a quick bow before exiting as quietly as he had entered.

"I prefer coffee in the morning," commented the Sheik languidly as he gestured Elizabeth to a chair beside his. Wordlessly she sat, unsure how to react to the man's mercurial nature. "May I pour you a cup?"

Elizabeth shook her head. "Coffee is too strong for me."

- The Sheik of Araby -

"Then I shall have Gaston make your English tea," the Sheik replied, unperturbed. At that moment the French servant reappeared, breakfast tray in hand. "Ah, Gaston. Tea for Madame."

With another silent bow, the servant was gone. Elizabeth mused that he must fear the Sheik as much as she did. Was there no one who could stand up to this man?

The Sheik returned to his newspaper. It was a Paris paper, and a few weeks old. As he studied the paper, Elizabeth had her first chance to study him. His face was bright and recently clean-shaven. He was fully dressed in crisp white swaths of cloth according to his fashion, and wearing his customary head covering tied with a braided rope of gold thread and camel hair. His large hands handled his small coffee cup expertly, and his face was untroubled. He seemed to have forgotten both her and the colt he had just conquered. Elizabeth's tea arrived as quickly and silently as her breakfast.

"This is *my* tea!" she exclaimed, tasting it. She had almost managed to forget the sight of Ibraheim Omair's body falling from his saddle as he defended her uncle's caravan. The Sheik looked up, meeting her eyes imperturbably.

"Naturally," he replied.

Elizabeth stared blankly into her teacup.

"What is to become of me?" she asked quietly.

Her companion laid down his newspaper, folding it neatly next to his plate.

"There is no need to think of that," he said sternly. "You will be well provided for. There are books to entertain you. Perhaps you may even ride with Gaston, when I am away."

Tears began to gather in Elizabeth's eyes. The Sheik saw them, and stood up. He clasped his hands behind his back and paced away from her.

"Tears do not become you," he said quietly, voice implacable.

"I cannot ignore the insult that has been visited upon me, Sir," Elizabeth replied, drying her eyes with the back of her hand.

"The insult!" the Sheik cried, spinning around to face her. In one quick motion he was beside her chair and had pulled her to her feet, strong hands grasping her arms so tightly it hurt. He glared down at her, his dark eyes burning. The instant Elizabeth raised her frightened eyes to his, he lowered his head to hers and kissed her, hard.

Elizabeth's first instinct was to pull away, but his iron grasp immobilized her. She turned her head, breaking the kiss, but a moment later he had shifted her body to the control of one great arm and pulled her face back to his with the other. His lips seared against her flesh as he took from her what he wanted. In another instant, she was free. He thrust her back towards her chair, where she sat stunned.

In two strides he was at the door of the tent. He paused, and threw back at her: "Now I have insulted you."

And then he was gone.

Elizabeth put her hand to her swollen lips. She could taste him. Only then did she notice that her teacup had fallen from her hands onto the intricately wrought table and shattered into a thousand splintered shards.

Chapter 5

The Sheik did not return that night, nor the next. Elizabeth's stomach soon ceased to turn each time she heard a horse reined in outside the tent, and she grew accustomed to Gaston's punctual service. Three times each day a meal was brought to her, each morning's breakfast with a fresh cup of her own British tea sitting quietly beside her plate.

The daytime hours passed with painful sluggishness. Elizabeth had tried, once, to leave the tent. A guard stood outside.

The night of the Sheik's sudden departure, Zilah prepared Elizabeth's bath as she had the night before. The silence was oppressive. Elizabeth decided to use her broken French to ask the girl about herself.

"Zilah," Elizabeth said, her voice crisp in the quiet of the tent. Zilah raised her head from her task of pouring oils into the steaming bath water, her brown eyes bright and large. She nodded her head in acknowledgement.

"How did you come to serve the Sheik?"

"I have always served the Sheik," replied Zilah softly, resuming her preparations.

"Does your family live with the tribe?" she asked at last.

The girl stopped once more, delicate hands paused above the water as though time had frozen.

"My family is dead," she replied quietly.

"I am sorry," Elizabeth said, saddened to have pained the girl. "How long ago?"

"Eleven years."

"You must have been a child!" Elizabeth exclaimed.

"Yes," Zilah replied slowly. "I was spared."

"Spared—" Elizabeth repeated. "You don't mean...your family was murdered?"

"In a raid, they were killed." Zilah seemed to have forgotten her discomfort, and answered matter-of-factly.

"Invaders came to the camp?"

"No, no," Zilah corrected. "It was the Sheik who raided my tribe. The father of the young Sheik." Zilah made an expansive gesture, to indicate the current owner of all that surrounded them.

"And you were taken, to serve him?" Elizabeth's horror was growing.

"By any other Sheik, I would have been left to die."

"Perhaps you would have preferred it!" Elizabeth cried, her own indignation emerging.

Zilah shook her head silently. She seemed to think for a moment.

"I was a girl-child, and of no value. I was taken, and fed, and cared for by the women of the Sheik's tribe. I have always been treated well, and the Sheik has forgiven my wrongs as no other would have."

"Your wrongs!" Elizabeth exclaimed. "You cannot mean your capture?"

Zilah looked down, studying the thick carpet as she paused in thought.

"No," she replied. "I betrayed the Sheik, once."

Elizabeth frowned, confused. "In what way?"

"There was a man," said the servant at last. "We were children together. When I was fifteen the old Sheik died, and the tribe was in confusion. He persuaded me to help him enter this tent. He told me that he loved me, and I believed his words. I followed him as he went to Ahmed's bedside, and raised a knife above the new Sheik's heart. I cried out, and Ahmed woke. They fought, nearly to the death. At last Ibraheim – "

"Ibraheim!" cried Elizabeth.

"Yes," continued Zilah. "His name was Ibraheim Omair. He broke away at last and held his knife to my throat. He told Ahmed he would kill me if he did not let him go. He spat on me and cursed me for my warning cry. Ahmed told him to leave and never come back. As Ibraheim pushed me away his knife slashed me here."

Zilah raised the dark curtain of her hair, revealing a thin white

49

line that trailed from beneath her left ear and along her jaw nearly to her chin. Elizabeth drew in a breath as she beheld the result of Omair's violence.

"The Sheik tended to my wounds, and told me as I cried that my heart would heal, and that I would love again. He trusted me still, and never blamed me for what I had done. He was correct. My life is good again."

Elizabeth leaned over and grasped the girl's slim brown hand in hers. "Are you certain, Zilah? That this life is good?"

Zilah squeezed the hand that clasped hers, her eyes alight. "Oh yes," she replied. "A life lit by love must always be good. For that I thank Allah."

Elizabeth raised her eyebrows. "So you did love again. Are you married?"

"Not yet," Zilah said shyly, drawing her hand away. She gestured to the readied bath. "Madame."

The following morning found Elizabeth pacing like an animal. There was no escape from the tent, and her mind was filled with excruciating worry for her family. Her elder sister, Jane, would be hurt the most should news of what had happened reach them. She and Jane were closest in age, and in disposition. Elizabeth was livelier and more boyish, but she and Jane were considered within the family and without to be the most sensible of the five sisters. How

50

- The Sheik of Araby -

she wished she were at home with dear Jane! Elizabeth recalled the
ill-hidden sorrow of Jane's face as her carriage pulled away from
Longbourn, and tears sprang to her eyes. She could never have
known where the journey would take her.

Frustrated, Elizabeth wandered to the bookshelf at the edge
of the largest room. To her surprise, it was full to bursting with a
wealth of diverse titles in French, Latin, English and Arabic. Well-
worn covers revealed the favorites of their owner, with pages marked
by threads of braided camel hair and tight notes written in an elegant hand in some of the margins. A full section of books had one
author: C. M. Bingley. The name sounded somewhat familiar, but
Elizabeth could not place it. The titles revealed a mix of subjects,
from cultural monographs to novels. Many took place in the Arab
world. Thumbing through one of the novels, sentence after sentence caught Elizabeth's eye. Interest piqued, she returned to the
flyleaf in order to begin reading from the beginning. There another
surprise awaited her. The book was inscribed, the date only a year
past. *To my dear friend Ahmed, it read. With thanks for another splendid so-
journ. Yours affectionately, Charles Bingley.* The words tumbled through
Elizabeth's mind. *"My dear friend Ahmed."* The phrase repeated itself
in her head. How could the author address that Arab brute with
such affectionate familiarity? The language must be overwrought,
or condescending somehow. Perhaps the Sheik had begged the author to come, since there was no culture to be had within his beck
and call. But no, that would further admit that the Sheik craved culture. Elizabeth simply could not reconcile the taciturn, selfish man
who had brazenly kidnapped her as the "dear friend" of a respected
author. A quick look through the other Bingley books revealed a

51

trend—affectionate notes to his dear friend, over a period of at least ten years.

Forcing herself to push her confusion aside, Elizabeth turned to the opening chapter of the novel she had first opened and began to read.

Hours later, Elizabeth's reverie was broken by the silent motion of Gaston pulling aside the door of the tent and entering with her dinner. After placing the tray on the low table, he made to bow and retreat as was his custom.

Still startled by her sudden reemergence into her own world, Elizabeth stopped him with a word. He halted, bowing once more and awaiting her orders

"Have you duties to perform elsewhere, Gaston?" she asked quickly.

"Nothing to speak of, Madame," he replied. "What is your desire?"

"Will you join me for my meal?"

"I regret, Madame, that I have already dined."

"Are you trying to say that your master would not permit us to share the meal?"

Gaston's expression changed, a hint of a smile barely perceptible.

"No, Madame," he answered. "I have already dined."

Elizabeth sighed. She glanced down at the book, open in her hands.

"Have you met Monsieur Bingley, Gaston?" she asked.

"*Oui*, Madame, quite frequently."

"How long have you served your master?"

"Fifteen years, Madame."

"Fifteen!" Elizabeth cried. "You must have been very young indeed."

"I was twenty-five when I began to serve Monseigneur the Sheik. My brother Henri and I had been forced to retire early. We were horse jockeys."

Elizabeth smiled as she imagined the young Gaston atop a hurtling steed. It certainly explained his tight, compact frame. "Is your brother in France still?"

"No, Madame, in England." At this Gaston cracked a true grin. "He is personal valet to Monsieur Bingley."

Elizabeth's surprised pause was just enough opportunity for Gaston to make a quick bow and his exit. Alone again, she reviewed her conversation with the man. His odd sense of humor appealed greatly to her sensibilities. He seemed a quick, intellectual fellow, and his apparent loyalty to the Sheik was beyond what she would have believed. It seemed to be based in camaraderie rather than fear, as she had early supposed. The more she learned, the less of what she thought she knew about the Sheik seemed possible.

- Lavinia Angell -

Chapter 6

With the setting of the sun each evening, Elizabeth counted another day against her planned month in the desert and mourned her captivity. The time passed slowly. Her days were filled with amusements of her own creation, as the Sheik did not seem to have thought twice about her empty hours. She read for most of the mornings, and eventually procured some needlework from Zilah to pass the days. The materials were unfamiliar—metal threads and beads which Zilah showed her how to loop into a tapestry of fantastical beauty—but the motions were the same as the needlework she had done in the parlor at Longbourn. Elizabeth was even able to convince Zilah to sit with her as they pulled needle in and out of cloth, talking amiably. By a combination of French and Arabic translation and gestures, Zilah learned passable English in a surprisingly short amount of time. Soon they were conversing in a halting manner on any number of topics.

The Sheik did not return, and no one seemed to think anything of his lengthy absence. Each day began as the last, with Gaston's faithful service of breakfast.

One morning Elizabeth was greeted by the sight of her riding costume, cleaned and pressed, laid out beside her breakfast tray. As if by magic, Gaston appeared with her morning cup of tea. She took it gratefully and shot a questioning look at the valet.

"Monseigneur has sent word, Madame, that you may ride today if you so wish."

At once the thought of freedom set Elizabeth's heart to a furious crescendo. She tried as best she could to maintain her composure.

"Alone?" she asked calmly.

"No, Madame," Gaston replied. "Never alone. I shall ride with you."

"Thank you, Gaston," Elizabeth said evenly. "Will ten o'clock be convenient?"

With a bow of assent he was gone, and Elizabeth was left to study the face of the silver clock that ticked upon a delicate table at the edge of the tent. She had been given an opportunity. It would not go to waste.

At ten o'clock Elizabeth found herself being boosted into the saddle of the very horse that had last carried her in a headlong gallop away from the chaos of the besieged caravan. She patted the familiar head soothingly, wondering quietly if the horse had fared better than she in their shared captivity.

The Arab who had led the horse to her handed her the reins. She recognized him as the handsome young companion who had tauntingly spoken over the Sheik's shoulder before the gambling hall, prompting Ahmed's curt dismissal of her beauty. Yusef, he had called the young man.

"Lujine is a fine mount. She suits you?" asked the Arab in passable French.

"Perfectly," replied Elizabeth perfunctorily. As she grasped the horse's reins, a sudden chill rippled through her. She lowered her gaze to look the handsome young man directly in the eyes. Slowly, she spoke. "Why did you call her Lujine?"

The young Arab laughed. "It means Shining Silver," he answered. "And describes her very well."

"No," Elizabeth interrupted. "I mean, how do you know that she is named so?"

A sudden flush spread over the young features and he looked away, conscious of having misspoken.

"The horse belongs to the Sheik," he said. Without another word he struck Lujine's firm flank, jolting the horse into motion. Elizabeth could hear Gaston's trailing curses directed at the young man as she struggled to control her headstrong mount. Within moments the beast was tamed, and Gaston sidled up to her on his own horse.

"A thousand apologies, Madame," he offered.

Elizabeth was unmoved. She was glad of the young man's misstep, which had revealed the full extent of his master's perfidy. All had been arranged. She recalled with perfect clarity the sinking moment that Lujine had responded to her master's whistle and halted, leaving her charge open to his assault. The Sheik held everything in the palm of his hand. Every man, horse and camel in this camp was broken to his will. All except her. With a whispered oath, Elizabeth thanked providence for the further reason to carry out her plan without an inkling of remorse.

Gaston close by her side, the pair started into the desert. The sun blazed upon them, wearying the Frenchman but only invigorating Elizabeth's tensed body. They rode for miles, the camp long disappeared behind them and only the open desert ahead.

"Madame," cried Gaston at last, trailing behind Elizabeth's resilient mount. "We must return."

Affecting disappointment, Elizabeth rounded her horse and returned to the spot where Gaston had paused.

"Very well," she sighed, pulling her handkerchief from her sleeve and lifting her helmet from her mass of curls to mop her brow. Suddenly the handkerchief slipped from her grasp and fluttered to the sand. She made to dismount, but Gaston stopped her with a gesture. Ever eager to serve, the French valet clambered from his own horse and began to trudge toward the flimsy white square.

In an instant, Elizabeth raised her crop and brought it down full force on the rump of Gaston's mount. The beast bolted, in mere moments speeding beyond the reach of either. The crop came down next on the frenzied Lujine, who, far from spent, broke into a forceful gallop. Ignoring the shocked cry of the betrayed valet, Elizabeth lowered her head and urged Lujine forward with whispered entreaties. The dust that insinuated itself into her mouth and nostrils tasted only of freedom, and minutes later the Frenchman was a speck on the distant horizon.

Horse and rider pushed hard for as long as the horse could bear before Elizabeth reined the beast to a stop. Desert stretched, vast and awful, in every direction. As she sipped the tiniest drop of moisture from her water skin before wetting Lujine's tongue and dusty nose, Elizabeth felt for the first time since setting out the very real fear that she would die, and soon. Pushing down the panicked knot that rose in her throat, she spoke softly to the horse.

"Come, sweet silvery beast," she asked. "Do you know the way to Biskra?"

She briefly considered giving the horse her head, but feared that the beast would only return her to their shared captor. The sun had fallen from its peak in the sky, and from its angle Elizabeth determined that she had been riding roughly north. So much the better she thought. At least I shall know that I am not journeying to the heart of Africa. As soon as Lujine's sides ceased to heave and her hooves became restless once again, Elizabeth coaxed her forward. Northward. To England.

Lujine had begun to slow.

- Lavinia Angell -

Pulling the mare to a halt in the meager shadow of a small outcropping of rock, Elizabeth lifted her veil and reached for her canteen. A shake confirmed what she had feared; it was empty. Even so, she pulled the cork and turned the canteen upside down over her cupped hand. A solitary drop dampened the dusty palm, darkening her skin in a tiny oasis of moisture. Unable to resist, Elizabeth touched her cracked lips to the spot. The water was hot, negating any satisfaction she might have gained from it.

"What are we to do?" she asked, leaning to whisper softly into the horse's ear. Lujine tossed her head wearily, sides still heaving between her rider's knees. Elizabeth stroked the glistening mane as she surveyed the darkening horizon.

At first, she was certain that her exhausted mind was betraying her. A dark line had appeared where sand met sky. Elizabeth's first thought was of a city, but her hopes were dashed when the shape grew larger, moving towards her slightly and to the west across the horizon. It must be a band of horses or camels. Elizabeth forced herself to use caution. A band of horses on the desert could as well be marauders as traders or pilgrims. She had learned that lesson well.

"We shall have to chance it, Lujine," Elizabeth said aloud. "Just a bit further, my dear."

Lujine was roused to a slow pace, which was good enough. The distance between the lone horse and rider and their salvation was closing. Soon, individual horsemen could be distinguished, their white burnouses flying behind them. They were traveling fast.

As the riders approached, seemingly ever quicker, Elizabeth's breath caught in her chest. Without a sound she wheeled her horse and headed back toward the outcropping. With any luck, she and her light-colored horse had not been seen.

It was too much to hope. The towering leader signaled his men to hold back, speeding alone instead after the solitary fugitive.

Dismounted and ducked behind a rock, Elizabeth knew at once that all hope was lost. She squeezed her eyes shut, pushing from her mind the punishments that were sure to be visited upon her once she was recovered. Lujine perked her ears at the sound of the approaching stallion, and Elizabeth had to forcibly hold her back at the sound of the whistle.

"Elizabeth!"

The voice was caught by the sand and wind and reached Elizabeth's ears half-formed. She pressed her lips tightly together, stroking Lujine's muzzle.

"Elizabeth!" It was closer now, and the urgency in the tone became more apparent. A minute or two passed, seeming an eternity.

"Are you alright?" came the voice, closer still. He was almost upon her. Elizabeth stayed silent.

"Are you armed?" asked the voice, hesitatingly.

Elizabeth tried to wet her lips to speak, but her parched tongue would not permit it. Her voice cracked as she forced a reply from her throat.

"Yes," she lied. "Stay back."

A moment's pause.

"I do not believe you," returned the voice with sinister inflection.

At once a long shadow fell into her vision, followed by its owner. The Sheik was tall and terrible, his face contorted into a scowl. Elizabeth knew she could not deceive him, so she dropped her hands to her sides. He strode to her and grasped her at once by the arm, his large hand closing tightly around her bicep. His face was dusty, with cracks of clean skin showing in the creases by his eyes. Beneath his cold gaze his mouth was curled, almost as though emotion was emerging of its own accord and against his express wishes.

"Where is Gaston?" he asked icily.

"I do not know," replied Elizabeth, voice shaking. All her mind could comprehend was the heat of his nearness and the iron clasp of his hand on her arm.

"Did you ride out together?"

"Yes," answered Elizabeth, meeting his gaze with courage she only half-felt. "I whipped his horse and left him in the desert."

The Sheik's eyes narrowed.

"How far from camp?"

"Miles."

"How long ago?"

"Perhaps seven hours."

Elizabeth flinched as the Sheik's other hand lifted suddenly, certain that a blow was coming. With shock, Elizabeth opened her eyes to see that it merely grasped Lujine's bridle. The Sheik's expression softened.

"I will never strike you, Elizabeth," he said quietly, a look that resembled hurt crossing his face.

Elizabeth had no reply, her mind still focused on the grip on her arm. She glanced at it unconsciously, and the Sheik's eyes followed her gaze. Immediately the pressure slackened, and his touch became more of a caress than a restraint.

"What would have happened if I had not come upon you?" he asked softly, entreaty in his eyes.

Elizabeth raised a confused countenance to his. "You did not follow me?"

The Sheik gave the slightest shake of his head. "We were returning to camp. I can recognize any of my horses from a mile's distance." He released her arm and ran a hand through his dark brown hair. "You cannot imagine my surprise to see you here."

His hand fell to his side, clenching and unclenching uselessly as he stared at the dust between their feet. Suddenly the tanned hand was lifted to Elizabeth's face, pushing her chin up to force her to look at him. His dark eyes were serious and sad.

"There is an enemy rallying at the northern border of my territory. To encounter him would be, for you, a fate worse than death."

Understanding instantly, Elizabeth averted her eyes from his.

The hand that cupped her chin moved to her cheek, thumb passing gently over the soft round of her skin. Looking up, Elizabeth realized that his gaze had traveled to her mouth. Nervously, she passed her tongue over the cracked crescent of her upper lip.

The tiniest hint of a smile crossed the tall man's features. Without a word he leaned down to meet her upturned face. He hesitated, just inches from her, eyes meeting hers in silent entreaty. Elizabeth closed her eyes, surrendering herself to the sensation of his warm, soft lips brushing lightly against hers. One arm came about her, pulling her close to his large form. The other entwined in the trailing curls at the nape of her neck. His kiss deepened, soft lips pressing against hers and even taking her lower lip gently between his. Elizabeth was frozen, not resisting nor participating. Suddenly she was released.

"Are my kisses so repulsive to you?" he asked.

Elizabeth opened her eyes and took in the man who had once seemed so impenetrable. The expression in his eyes showed but a glimmer of hope that she would reply in the negative.

"Yes," she said, knowing at once that it was a lie.

"Come," he said, turning from her and recapturing Lujine's bridle. His eyes turned stony, and he seemed to look through her. "We must pray that Gaston has fared as well as you have."

As soon as the fires of the camp were in sight a rider galloped out to meet the Sheik's party. It was Yusef, the young man whom the Sheik had left in command of the camp in his absence.

"My Sheik!" he cried, approaching.

"Where is Gaston?" asked the Sheik immediately, eyes afire.

Yusef shook his head. "His mount returned alone some hours ago. There is no sign of Madame or Gaston."

Elizabeth's horse nudged forward, revealing her to the young Arab. His eyes widened.

"Madame," he said, bowing. "I am most pleased to see that you are safe."

"As are we all," added the Sheik, voice cold. Elizabeth could discern no trace of the man who had kissed her so tenderly only hours before.

"Take Madame to my tent," the Sheik ordered. "The camp shall not rest until Gaston is located."

With a deep bow, Yusef took hold of Lujine's bridle and guided the weary beast homeward. Elizabeth's mind went at once to the French valet, stranded in the desert. The thirst and heat of her own hours on the plain had solidified in her mind what a painful death she might have caused Gaston, and for the first time began to fear for him. The Sheik's worry was contagious. Suddenly it occurred to her that if she had caused the death of his friend, her life might well be the price. A cold shiver ran through her as she contemplated that his might be the only kiss she was ever to know.

As soon as she entered the tent Elizabeth cast off her filthy riding clothes and wrapped a silk robe around her dust-encrusted body. Crossing to the inner chamber, she was surprised to see the coverlet of the bed turned back and her nightdress set out, just as it had been each night. It was difficult to believe that only twelve hours had passed since she left the camp on Lujine's back. The day had seemed a week. Running an impatient hand through her curls, Elizabeth rang the small bell for Zilah. Ordinarily she eschewed the device, but she was in great need of a bath that only Zilah could prepare. The girl appeared almost instantly.

"Madame!" she cried, running lightly to Elizabeth and impulsively throwing her arms about her. She released her quickly and stood back, eyes shining. "You are safe!"

"For the moment," replied Elizabeth solemnly, refusing to allow herself to forget the punishment she would receive.

"Yusef was so fearful," continued the girl. "When Gaston's horse appeared – "

"You spoke to Yusef?" asked Elizabeth, curious how news of her escapade had spread.

Zilah dropped her gaze to the floor. "He asked me if I had seen you," she said curtly. "What does Madame wish? A bath?"

"Yes, if you would be so kind," Elizabeth sighed, sitting heavily at the edge of the bed. Zilah went to work quickly and efficiently, producing everything needed for Elizabeth to scrub the stain of her betrayal from her body.

Emerging from the water, Elizabeth patted her hair dry with a cotton cloth and slipped into a fresh robe. Her riding clothes and helmet had vanished, replaced by the toiletries she would need for the evening. Never could Elizabeth remember being so doted upon.

Approaching the outer curtain, Elizabeth realized that she was not alone in the tent. Outside the soft footfalls of the Sheik could be heard, a familiar pacing tread on the deep carpet. She parted the curtains quietly, but as always managed to alert him to her presence. He turned and regarded her thoughtfully.

"I wonder," he said at last. "Is one life worth that of another?"

Cold fingers seized Elizabeth's heart. "Is Gaston not returned?" she asked meekly.

"No," replied the Sheik, turning on his heel. "He is not."

Elizabeth slipped into the room and sat quietly on a cushioned lounge. The Sheik seemed to have forgotten her, resuming his pacing. Occasionally he would stop, sigh, and run his hand through his ruffled mane.

"It is my fault," Elizabeth said at last, looking at her hands.

The Sheik's pacing halted, his hands clasped sternly behind his back.

"Yes," he answered. "It is."

"You ask if one life is worth the price of another," began Elizabeth. "I believe it is."

The Sheik raised an eyebrow expectantly.

Elizabeth forced herself to continue. "My life cannot equal that of your friend and trusted servant. Despite that, I have done wrong and am prepared to pay for my actions."

He crossed the room at a leisurely rate and, to her astonishment, sat beside her.

"You believe that I would kill you, purely for revenge?" he asked evenly.

"Is it not your way?" Elizabeth questioned softly.

"It is the Arab way," the Sheik replied thoughtfully. "But you are not an Arab."

Elizabeth did not respond.

"In a way," continued the Sheik, almost to himself, "neither am I."

"What do you mean?" asked Elizabeth, intrigued. The Sheik seemed to escape a momentary reverie, bringing his voice to usual volume once more.

"Nothing of consequence," he asserted. "Merely that in many ways my leadership varies from that of other Sheiks."

Hesitant to provoke him, but eager to hear his reasons, Elizabeth decided to question him further. "You do not use corporal punishment?"

Surprised, the Sheik raised his head. "Of course I do."

"Then how—"

"You misunderstand," interrupted the Sheik. "It is difficult to explain to one who was not born here, but I shall try. Without the threat of such action, my authority would collapse. There is no law here, Miss Bennet. The tribes are unreachable by courts, by justice as you know it. In the desert, the law must be upheld by an agreement between all citizens. The transgressor knows, without a doubt, that death may result. The Sheik knows that his duty is to protect his people by removing a threat to them or to the peace. In this way, the people of the desert avoid anarchy and violence."

"But you are something of a despot, are you not?" asked Elizabeth, forgetting her fear for the moment. He seemed accessible, and far from the judge, jury and executioner he described.

The Sheik responded with a wry smile. "Would you care to hold an election, Miss Bennet?" In her silence, he continued. "In any case the people would elect the strongest man, for he is the only one who can protect them."

Elizabeth was silent for a long minute, and the Sheik turned his head back to the flap of the tent, waiting for the face he most hoped to see. Elizabeth was ashamed of herself, more heartily than she had thought she could ever be.

"Is it expected that I should die if Gaston does not return?" she asked at last.

"Perhaps," said the Sheik, eyes distant. "But I do not think he would want such a thing."

"He is a kind man," Elizabeth said quietly, eyes filling with tears.

"He has brightened my days."

The Sheik seemed to see Elizabeth's tears without turning to face her.

"Could you never be happy here?" he asked sadly.

She turned her face away, shamed that tears ran freely down her cheeks. She clasped her hands tightly in her lap, wringing the fabric of her robe in frustration.

"I ask too much, I know," he said. "Do not answer. I am too selfish a creature to let you go, and if you do not tell me I may hope that you are not as miserable as you are."

Elizabeth opened her mouth to reply, but the Sheik's grasp on the arm of the divan had tightened as his body coiled to spring into action. A commotion sounded outside the tent, and a moment later the flap was thrust back.

"Monsieur!" cried Gaston frantically. "*Mon ami!*" exclaimed the Sheik, gathering the Frenchman into a warm Arab embrace. He held him at arm's length and examined the damage.

"I am alright," reassured the servant, waving away the Sheik's attentions. He caught sight of Elizabeth over the Sheik's shoulder.

"Oh, Madame!" he cried, emotion threatening to overtake his countenance. A flurry of French escaped his lips, of which Elizabeth only caught a word or two. The Sheik placed his hand on Gaston's shoulder, calming him with a soothing tone.

"Gaston," Elizabeth ventured at last, approaching the pair cautiously. "There is no way for me to apologize for the danger to which I exposed you—"

"I believe, Miss Bennet," interjected the Sheik, "That Monsieur Gaston was primarily concerned for your safety. He knows of the enemy nearby as well as I, which he says was the reason he stopped you where he did."

"I am ashamed of myself," Elizabeth repeated.

A twinkle appeared in Gaston's tired eyes. "Forgive me, Monsieur, but I must say to the lady that she hardly acted unexpectedly, though with more courage and deviousness than I should have imagined."

"Courage she does not lack," said the Sheik dryly, regarding Elizabeth. He turned back to the desert-weary servant. "Did you walk back? The whole journey?"

"*Oui*, Monsieur..."

The Sheik and his valet launched into a fast-paced French narrative to which Elizabeth could contribute nothing. Their voices faded from her ears as she removed herself to her own thoughts.

Elizabeth retreated quietly into the bedroom, heart both gladdened and pained at Gaston's safe return. She could see now that his immediate forgiveness was a wound she would have to live with for the remainder of her life. His hatred, or her death, would have been a blessing in comparison to looking each morning into the generous eyes of the man she had left to die.

Chapter 7

E lizabeth woke with a start. Her first conscious thought was that she was not alone. Indeed, the weight that fell across her shoulder was the pressure of an arm, limp in sleep, draped around her protectively. Its owner did not seem to have been awakened by the motion of her surprise, and for a moment Elizabeth was able to study her position without disturbing it. Her head lay on the Sheik's great bare shoulder, her cheek nestled into the hollow beneath his collar bone. Even more shocking, her arm was draped in a similar manner across his broad chest. Her nascent awareness of the feeling of his warm, smooth skin under her arm inspired an instantaneous and powerful blush to creep up her neck and into her cheeks. From her position tucked underneath his chin, she could see nothing of her companion's face. Perhaps it was better that way. With a sharp intake of breath, she extracted herself gently from their tangle of limbs. Leaving the Sheik sleeping she retreated to the washroom, the only place to which she could escape in order to form a coherent thought.

He must have come to bed very late, Elizabeth thought. She had fallen into a deep, exhausted slumber as soon as his voice and Gaston's passed out of the tent and left her alone in silence. It was the first time he had slept at the camp since her first dreadful night. With a shudder, Elizabeth again wondered why he had not made good on his sinister promise of that first day.

Quietly Elizabeth dressed and made ready for the day, hoping against hope that she would not have to face him when she reemerged.

He was not there.

Unsure if it was relief or disappointment that crushed her spirits, Elizabeth passed to the bed in which they had both taken their rest. The impression of his head remained in the pillow, and the coverlet was thrown back as he must have cast it from his body to rise. Elizabeth ran her hand across the sheet where he had lain. It was cool to the touch.

Elizabeth's head snapped up at the sound of shouting somewhere outside the tent. A great crowd seemed to be gathered nearby, and a disagreement was being debated in loud Arabic. Following the sound, Elizabeth pulled back the large, heavy exterior flap and stepped outside. The guard who had stood by the door in the Sheik's absence was gone. Indeed, the camp seemed deserted but for the cacophony of voices.

- The Sheik of Araby -

Crossing the camp cautiously, Elizabeth found herself drawn to the source of the noise. The edge of a large crowd was pressing forward to some spectacle, and Elizabeth managed to insinuate herself into it without being noticed.

At the center of the throng towered the Sheik himself, clean-shaven and impeccably groomed. He stood solidly, arms crossed before him, face unreadable. Elizabeth gasped as she realized that Zilah knelt at his feet, prostrate and begging. The source of the conflict seemed to lie with her, as various tribe members gestured and shouted their opinions as to what the Sheik should do with her.

The Sheik spoke slowly and evenly in measured Arabic, immediately silencing the crowd. He seemed to ask a question of Zilah, who responded by clasping her hands in silent entreaty. He then raised his head to address another man, a bearded tribesman whose clothing was rich but still below the luxury of that of the Sheik himself. The Sheik's hand rested casually on the butt of the pistol he kept thrust in his sash, fingers tapping idly at the gem-encrusted grip as he listened calmly to the tribesman's testimony. The tribesman's purse was produced, and coin was noisily displayed.

A moment later, the Sheik seemed to have come to a decision. At his call, Yusef stepped forward from the throng. With a barely perceptible gesture, the Sheik motioned Zilah to her feet. Yusef crossed to her and spoke a few words, answering a question put to him by his master. The Sheik spoke at last, prompting a whoop from the crowd and a swift motion from Yusef, who pulled his purse from beneath his robes and bowed as he placed a sum of coin at the Sheik's feet, then threw his arm around Zilah and quickly pulled her away from the scene. The bearded tribesman spat on the ground, gathering his gold and slinking away. The crowd dispersed, and the Sheik's gaze fell immediately on Elizabeth, standing silently where she had witnessed all. He scooped the coin at his feet into his own purse and crossed to her.

"Miss Bennet," he said formally, effecting a slight bow.

"What happened?" Elizabeth asked, unable to tame her curiosity. The pain on Zilah's face had struck her to the heart, and she was unsure if she was ever to see the girl again.

"You have shown remarkably little interest in the mating habits of the Arabs thus far," the Sheik replied evasively, prompting Elizabeth's ears to pinken. "I am certain that the details of the dispute you just witnessed would repulse you equally."

"Are you implying – " began Elizabeth, stuttering. "Was that man attempting to buy Zilah?"

"By right, she is my property." The Sheik's eyes were dark and challenging.

"Because your father murdered her family and kidnapped her?" spat Elizabeth, rage rising.

"Would you prefer she had died with them?" demanded the Sheik.

"Do not ask me my opinion regarding the relative merits of death and kidnapping, Sir. I fear it would not reflect well on you," warned Elizabeth, eyes alight.

"You have made that clear enough, Madam," growled the Sheik, body tensing.

"Should I prepare to be sold to another of your favorites? Perhaps Yusef merits another concubine. Then, at least, I could keep

- The Sheik of Araby -

Zilah company." The words flowed from Elizabeth's lips, her conscious mind heedless of what she said until she heard it herself.

The Sheik looked as though he had been slapped.

Elizabeth regarded him in triumph, hands clenched at her sides as the verbal blow she had delivered made contact with her foe. A moment later he had regained his composure.

"What is your price, Miss Bennet?" he asked steadily, eyes never leaving hers. Elizabeth flushed, willfully misunderstanding him.

"I do not comprehend your meaning," she said defiantly.

"But you do, Madam," he replied. "I refer to your dowry. Upon your marriage, what sum is your husband to receive in exchange for lessening the burden you place upon your parents?"

With utmost embarrassment, Elizabeth uttered the horrible words below her breath: "Fifty pounds, Sir."

The Sheik's even gaze bore into her, causing the blood to surge in her ears as she stood before him. At once she saw the vastness of the chasm between them. His empire was worth a fortune; her maidenhood could be had for fifty pounds.

"I must ask, Miss Bennet, that you refrain from commenting on that which you do not understand. It does no credit to either of us. Excuse me," he said shortly. "I have business to which I must attend."

Elizabeth watched the flutter of his white robes as he strode out of sight. With tears stinging in her eyes, she turned and returned to the tent.

To her great surprise, Zilah was waiting eagerly for her return. Instantly the girl crossed to Elizabeth and grasped both her hands.

75

"Madame!" she cried. "Where have you been? The most wonderful thing has happened!"

"Zilah, I—" Elizabeth stammered, unsure what to think of this reversal of emotion.

"Early this morning a man named Ghabah offered for me, promising the Sheik a great sum of gold to give me as a bride."

"The bearded man with the purse?" asked Elizabeth incredulously.

"You saw?" gaped Zilah. "Yes, that was he!"

"What did the Sheik do?" asked Elizabeth, dread forming in her mind that she had been very, very wrong about what had transpired.

"The Sheik asked me what were my wishes, and I begged him to let me stay free."

"I saw the man offer again," said Elizabeth.

"Yes, but the Sheik would not hear him. Then he told me that he would not let me remain free. I was so...helpless! So sad!"

"What then?"

"He called Yusef forward. He told us that he had seen the love between us, and asked Yusef what he should do."

A light entered Zilah's eyes as she spoke of Yusef, and Elizabeth was amazed she had not seen it before. With shame she realized that the Sheik knew better than she did what Zilah wished for most.

"Yusef asked for me," Zilah said giddily. "I am so happy! Many people were surprised, because Yusef may lead the tribe after the Sheik, and I am only a servant."

"But I saw Yusef give the Sheik a sum of coins. Why?"

Zilah looked, for the first time, as though Elizabeth had said something stupid. "It was the marriage tribute," she said impatiently.

"The Sheik said something. What was it?"

"He told all the people that we should never scorn love when Allah bestows it on two young people as He had done for us, for to do so would be ungrateful to Allah and unkind to those who love. I knew that the Sheik's kindness would not fail us. This Sheik is the kindest and most just of any in the desert, it is said."

"Congratulations, Zilah," Elizabeth said through tears, embracing the girl. "I shall miss you."

Zilah's eyes grew wide. "No, Madame! I may still serve you. Yusef will allow it."

Startled, Elizabeth realized that she had overlooked yet another cultural divide. "Will the Sheik?"

"Yes, of course," said Zilah, smiling broadly. "I wish you could be so happy as I, Madame."

"Thank you, Zilah," said Elizabeth softly. "So do I."

That night, Elizabeth was surprised to see the Sheik enter the washroom early in the evening. She heard the sound of the steaming bath water being poured, and wondered that she had never seen Gaston serve the same office for the Sheik as Zilah did for her.

Curiosity piqued, Elizabeth approached the flap separating the bedroom from the washroom. Unwilling to intrude, she hesitated. At that moment the flap was thrown back and she was nearly bowled over by the towering form of the Sheik himself. His long robes had been shed, leaving him in loose pants and a simple shirt of snow-white cotton. His sleeves were rolled past the elbow, strong tanned forearms glistening and wet. He seemed as surprised to meet Elizabeth as she was, but recovered his countenance at once.

"Miss Bennet," he acknowledged. "I was coming to find you."

Elizabeth was somewhat shocked at his civility, her conscience still reeling from the insult she had earlier laid at his door. She managed a curtsey in answer.

"I am afraid that Zilah will be unable to serve you tonight," continued the Sheik, looking at her earnestly. Elizabeth could bear no more.

"You must forgive me, Sir," she interrupted. "I cannot allow you to continue. Zilah explained all to me, and I am ashamed to think of what I assumed."

"I too have thought long on your condemnation of me," replied the Sheik. "Your assumption was natural, if too hasty. I cannot hold it against you."

"Then why were you—" began Elizabeth, confused.

"I have taken the liberty of preparing your bath myself," said the Sheik quickly, gesturing to the washroom.

Elizabeth was stunned. Indeed, this was the last action she had expected on his part. Was it possible that the time had finally come, that tonight would be the night he made her his own? His start was auspicious, if so.

- The Sheik of Araby -

"That is very kind of you, Sir," she stuttered.

The Sheik stood back to make way for her, diminishing, if only slightly, the impressive threat of his tall figure. Suddenly conscious of every motion of her body, Elizabeth lifted her chin and entered the washroom, from which emanated a magical array of spiced fragrance. Despite the welcoming sight of the bathtub, Elizabeth felt as though she were walking to her own execution. Would he strip her clothes from her? Would she try to stop him? Could she succeed?

Thoughts swimming, Elizabeth reached the bathtub and mechanically dipped her fingertips into the steaming water. It was perfect.

"I know that Zilah has a remarkable way with the bath," said the Sheik casually. At once a vision entered Elizabeth's mind: Zilah, soaping the Sheik's broad shoulders as he reclined. A surge of inexplicable jealousy sprang within her chest that she could force down only by remembering how wrong every assumption she had made about this man had been. The nearness of his form sent a heat through Elizabeth that she could only push down by clenching her wet fingertips against her palm, concentrating on the prick of her fingernails against the flesh there. *Am I insane?* Elizabeth asked herself wonderingly. *Is it possible that I am beginning to want this man?*

"...with cinnamon, as I was once shown long ago." The Sheik paused, apparently noticing the abstraction in Elizabeth's sightless eyes.

"Forgive me," Elizabeth said quickly. "Who taught you?"

The Sheik looked hard at Elizabeth, forcing a blush to rise to her cheeks. "My mother," he said at last.

79

Flustered, Elizabeth could only manage, "She possessed quite a talent. This concoction surpasses even Zilah's impressive creations."

The Sheik nodded his head in acknowledgement, and with a sinking sensation Elizabeth realized that he intended to remain while she undressed.

"I thank you," she said decisively. "That will be all."

Not a muscle of his imposing figure moved at her behest. His eyes were clapped upon her in rapt attention, but his face revealed nothing of the emotion behind his gaze.

"You will turn me away?" he asked innocently.

"My honor forbids otherwise."

A laugh crackled through the tension-filled atmosphere, his teeth bright against his dark skin. "You seem not to realize that I will do as I please," he reflected, amused.

"My courage always rises with every attempt to intimidate me," Elizabeth said forcefully, small feet planted firmly in place.

"You do find me intimidating, then?" mused the Sheik, a smile still lingering on his lips.

"Come, Sir," Elizabeth entreated. "We are each of an unsociable, taciturn nature, unwilling to speak unless we expect to say something that will amaze the whole room. Intimidation is an accepted weapon of the celebrated wit, and one that you at least are well aware lies within your arsenal."

"No great resemblance to your own character, I am sure."

"I am aware that my talents as a judge of character have been sorely lacking since my introduction to this place," Elizabeth conceded. "But you have not so much as attempted to make mine out, or you should have done as I first asked and returned me to my company, or killed me, for I shall never yield to you."

"I have never boasted to possess the discernment you claim," countered the Sheik calmly. "As you may be aware, I am rarely called upon to judge the nuance of my opponent's temperament. The glint of a sword brings out in a man all that need be known."

"It may well be so," she admitted. "I have not opened my heart and mind to your culture as well as I had hoped to, but I consider that to be my own failing, because I would not take the trouble of practicing."

"And you believe that I would do well to follow your edict and make out the characters of my fellow man?"

"Such an exploration need not stop at your fellow men," Elizabeth said pointedly.

"My emotions concerning you, Miss Bennet, are of a nature that prevents the objective calculation of your character."

Elizabeth's heart froze in her chest. She spoke slowly. "To what emotions do you refer?"

The Sheik eyed her thoughtfully.

"Fear not, Madam, that I will utter a word as hateful to you as 'love.' That emotion was stricken from my body long ago with the loss of someone I loved more than my own life."

Elizabeth released a breath that she had not realized she was holding. The Sheik continued, eyes never leaving hers.

"The nature of my interest in you, Miss Bennet, should be obvious. I desire you."

The hands that clasped her robe tightly around her body clenched even tighter. "If such was your goal, you have had ample opportunity, Sir."

"Indeed," replied the Sheik. "But I shall not take you by force. You will grow to love me. I shall make you love me, as I have done others before you. You will beg me to take you. And then, when you have given yourself to me, I shall tire of you. It is my curse that I want nothing I may take and desire only that which I may not."

Unspeakable horror crossed Elizabeth's features, blood draining from her face.

"You are a monster," she gasped.

"You are correct," replied the Sheik. With that he retreated, leaving Elizabeth alone in the perfumed den of the washroom. She fell back against the edge of the bathtub, unable to comprehend his words. She had come so close to caring for him. He must have seen it, somehow, and decided to extend his little game of cat-and-mouse. Hardening her resolve, Elizabeth vowed to push the Sheik from her mind and give him no satisfaction whatsoever. Her heart was her own, and she would never give him even the tiniest piece.

That night Elizabeth waited sleeplessly for the Sheik to join her in bed. It was only the second night since his return to camp, and his presence that morning had unnerved her. With a shudder she recalled the feeling of waking with his arms around her—and with her arms around him. In those first waking moments she had been unbelievably happy, until, of course, she realized in whose arms she lay.

The Sheik's words in the washroom as she stood clad only in her thin silk robe had reminded her of the thin line that separated his body from hers. His confidence that she would come to love him was hardly surprising, considering his egoistic behavior at every turn. What frightened Elizabeth, though, was that it seemed to be born of experience. He had mentioned that he had played this game before. In her innocence, Elizabeth wondered what he might do to her in order to invoke the love he promised she would come to feel for him.

As the night wore on, Elizabeth lay awake listening to the sound of the Sheik turning the pages of a book in the outer room. Occasionally the rasp of a match being struck reached her ears, followed by the subtle scent of the Turkish tobacco he favored. At last the lamps were extinguished, and she held her breath awaiting his introduction into the bed. She did not know what she would do, should he attempt to embrace her. Recalling the sensation of his kiss as they faced one another under the rocky outcropping, she brought her fingers to her mouth in memory. Her touch was cold on her own skin.

Minutes passed, and Elizabeth stared into the dark above her head.

Heart pounding against her chest, she pushed the heavy brocade cover off of her body and placed her bare feet on the thickly carpeted floor. A few steps brought her to the flap that separated them, and with trembling fingers she lifted the canvas silently.

Silver moonlight alone lit the large outer chamber, cast in stripes from tiny slits where the walls of the tent met the roof. He lay on the divan, one arm thrown over his face. His lower half was covered lightly by the thin cotton of his burnous, drawn over him against the chill of night. He had discarded his clothes on the chair nearby, crisp white fabric falling over the back like a waterfall in the darkened tent. His other hand lay gently over his heart, lightly touching the bare skin of his broad chest. With a gasp, Elizabeth let the flap fall.

Lightly slipping into the bed and between the silk sheets Elizabeth put her hand to her throat and calmed the quickened pulse that surged in her veins. At last the stillness of the room settled down upon her and she turned her face to the ceiling, eyes wide and unseeing in the pitch black of the darkened chamber. She curled her toes, stretched her body across the empty expanse of the large bed. As the satiny fibers slid across her taut body she inhaled suddenly, awakening desire insinuating itself into her consciousness. Tentatively she ran her hands over her arms, her neck, her breasts, rousing her own flesh to the light caress of her touch. Her hands trembled, paused, then clenched against themselves as her thoughts turned to the character of the man of whom she dreamed, the man whose hands she wished would run over her body as hers had done. Her mind could not go beyond the desire for his touch upon her flesh, beyond the tension that pooled in her stomach at the sight of his bared body. She knew that if he touched her, he would not stop.

Pulling the brocade cover over her once more, Elizabeth closed her eyes tightly for the first time that night. It was no use. All she could see was his body, bared before her, stretched on the divan as she sank into the feathers of his luxurious bed.

Chapter 8

The Sheik, now returned to camp, had taken over the responsibility of accompanying Elizabeth on her excursions into the desert. It was plain that he would abide no attempt to sway or elude him, so Elizabeth abandoned all hope of repeating her ill-fated escape. Each morning they met, exchanged pleasantries, and mounted their horses. The Sheik rode a powerful beast he called Shaitan, a magnificent jet-black Arabian whose back stood higher even than Elizabeth's head. Together they galloped in silence, giving the horses their heads, until the beasts and riders were winded and began to tire.

"It is a fine prospect, is it not?" asked the Sheik, breathing heavily, one morning as they reined in their mounts at the crest of a sun-drenched dune. The desert spread before them like an expanse of satin carelessly cast aside, wrinkled and creased with endless peaks of drifting sand. At the horizon the piercing blue of the Algerian sky met the blinding brightness of the sand in a crisp line blurred only slightly by undulating waves of heat rising from the dunes. Elizabeth felt that she should have been able to see all the way to England on a day like this one, the curve of the earth laid bare before her unending gaze.

"Very," she replied shortly. Tears threatened at her thoughts of home. She lifted her veil and pushed an errant curl away from her face, using the motion as an excuse to turn her gaze away from the Sheik's penetrating looks.

The Sheik uttered a low whistle, almost indiscernible, pricking Lujine's ears and prompting her to sidle closer to him where he sat mounted on Shaitan. Elizabeth, her unwilling burden, cast a disapproving glare at the instigator of the beast's motion.

"You might honor me with a compliment to the land I love," urged the Sheik, attempting to catch Elizabeth's eye. "You do think it beautiful, do you not?"

Irritated, Elizabeth refused to appease him. "A beautiful view cannot be improved upon by talking about it."

At her words a small smile appeared on the Sheik's lips, and he returned his gaze to the horizon.

"You would contend that there is no merit in the sharing of a stirring experience, then."

"Would you think the view any more or less beautiful if I agreed with your opinion of it?"

"The view would be no better," he said simply. "But I would

86

be pleased to see the pleasure in your eyes."

Elizabeth shot a glance at him, but his finely formed profile was turned to the distant horizon. But for his words, she would have thought herself forgotten.

"We should turn back," she said quickly, taking up Lujine's reins and pulling her about. With a soft click of his tongue the Sheik wheeled Shaitan around, then paused to allow Elizabeth to lead the way.

The trip back was more leisurely, and Elizabeth found herself curious about the Sheik's odd comments.

"Do you speak as a rule, Sir, when observing a fine prospect?" she asked, pulling Lujine back to trot alongside his mount.

"Indeed," replied the Sheik. "Yusef finds my exposition on a view quite enthralling."

Despite herself, Elizabeth let out a laugh. The Sheik turned to eye her carefully, regarding her pleasure with a concerned expression.

"Do not attempt to make me laugh, Sir, if you cannot bear the result," Elizabeth advised, dismayed at his silent reproof.

"I was not trying to make you laugh. I assure you that Yusef is an eager listener, and I an eager poet on the subject of a view," said the Sheik, a mischievous glint appearing in his eye.

"A shame," Elizabeth smiled. "For I dearly love to laugh, and have found too little exercise in it since..."

She stopped herself from uttering the words, but it was too late. The Sheik's face darkened and he nudged Shaitan into a burst of speed, leaving her to follow without another chance at speech. With a sigh Elizabeth turned her head to the west and regarded the slowly setting sun as it fell gently down the surface of the sky.

As the days wore on, Elizabeth found that the Sheik was not opposed to speaking on almost any subject she chose. As they paused at the end of their headlong gallop, he would often ask her a question or beg her opinion on an author or theory, and their meandering debates not infrequently led them all the way back to the camp. Though somewhat suspicious that she was being tested, Elizabeth answered his queries with as much spirit as she could muster, and found that their views rarely disagreed. He was in fact quite eloquent and knowledgeable on a variety of topics, and Elizabeth felt that even if they were to ride each day for the rest of their lives she would never truly plumb the depths of his mind.

After their ride the Sheik often lingered in the tent with her and engaged her in further conversation. Sitting comfortably in a chair at the edge of the room, he would light a cigarette and lean his towering form into a posture of catlike repose, idly staring at the ceiling as smoke curled up around him. Although her feelings were hardened against him Elizabeth felt privileged to see him thus, head bare and shirt open at the throat as he took his ease.

"Your command of Arabic at the door of the Club Mansur was quite impressive, Miss Bennet," he began one day a few minutes after they had taken their places in the large room of the tent.

"Do not tease me," Elizabeth pleaded, blushing.

The Sheik sat up and dropped his cigarette into an ashtray, allowing its smoke to rise unheeded from the golden cup.

"I do not tease," he said solemnly.

"Then I thank you," Elizabeth said dismissively, rising to take a book from the shelf.

"*Ketab*," he said suddenly. "I beg your pardon?" Elizabeth asked, turning to him in confusion. He gestured to the book she held.

"*Ketab*," she repeated, understanding, turning the book over in her hands. With a look at the Sheik, she pulled a second book from the shelf and placed it on top of the first.

"*Ketabani*," he said, eyes never leaving hers. "*Shokran*," she said softly. He nodded in acceptance of her thanks. "*Al'afw*," he replied.

One morning Elizabeth woke to the faint sound of a man singing. The voice was clear and true, though the song had a sad lilting melody.

Emerging from the bedroom as softly as she could, Elizabeth came upon the Sheik, dressing in the early morning light. He was singing lustily, voice caressing the tune. With a chill she realized that his was undoubtedly the voice she had heard below her window in Biskra, for the song was the very same.

Pale hands, pink-tipped,

like lotus buds that float
on those cool waters where
we used to dwell...

As his voice lingered on the final note, the Sheik seemed to wake from his reverie. Elizabeth tried to be surprised, but failed to be, at the knowledge that he had watched her at her balcony in Biskra. He turned to Elizabeth with a broad smile, the sight of which was so startling that she nearly took a step back.

"What wakes you so early?" she asked blankly, choosing to ignore the appealing sight of the dimples that had appeared on the Sheik's tanned cheeks.

"Ah!" he cried, elated. "I am riding out."

"Are we not to ride today?" asked Elizabeth dispiritedly.

The Sheik's grin was reduced to a mere smile and he advanced towards her, taking her small hands in his. "You will miss me, my sweet?"

She pulled her hands away. "I will miss the ride," she countered.

The Sheik tossed his head back and laughed aloud.

"Try though you might, you cannot quash my good spirits, my lady," he teased. "For I am riding to Biskra to meet my friend."

Elizabeth stood silently, eyes cast down. The Sheik's happy mood was anything but infectious.

"Will you not inquire of me which friend?" he prodded, lowering his head to better view Elizabeth's down-turned face.

"How should I know any of your friends?" demanded Elizabeth, annoyed. "The only person with whom I have seen you connected was the lady on your arm at the Commandant's dinner, and she thoughtfully neglected to introduce herself."

The Sheik sighed. "Ah yes. Caroline de Veilleux. Her manners leave something to be desired, it is true, but I tolerate her out of respect for her brother, my greatest friend and the man whom I meet today."

"A Frenchman?"

"*Mais non*, Mademoiselle," smiled the Sheik. "Both are English. Caroline married the Vicomte de Veilleux and travels often, though rarely in the company of her husband. Her brother is also an adventurer, and indeed you may know his work. He is called Charles Bingley."

"Charles Bingley!" Elizabeth cried in disbelief. Panic rose as she contemplated the idea of meeting the man. Before she knew what she was doing, she pleaded: "I beg you, Sir, do not force me to endure his company."

A shadow crossed the Sheik's countenance. "Do not be ridiculous. You shall play hostess to Mr. Bingley as you would any other guest of mine. I assure you his society is very pleasant."

"Please, Sir," Elizabeth begged, moving to clasp the Sheik's great hand. "You do not understand. I cannot abide to be seen by my countryman, slave to you as I am. He will know that we have shared a bed, and I could not bear the shame."

Brow darkening, the Sheik contemplated her plea. At last he spoke, carefully measured words that weighed heavily on Elizabeth's hopes.

"I had not considered that," he frowned. "Nonetheless, the fact remains that you belong to me. He shall see you, and you shall see him. You must make the best of it, for my plans are already settled."

"I beg you!" cried Elizabeth. "Stay with him in Biskra, or allow me to stay elsewhere in the camp. I cannot face him."

"My plans are settled," repeated the Sheik, eyes steely. "Be ready to receive us tonight."

With that he turned and was gone.

After the cacophony of the party's departure had settled down, Elizabeth continued to tread the large floor of the tent. His deafness to her pleas had saddened her more than she could say. She had sensed a modicum of respect in his manner towards her of late, but it was clear that he had never been denied any whim. At last Elizabeth fell into a chair, head resting wearily in her hands. The world she had once known had faded to the back of her memory over the weeks of her captivity, but the prospect of meeting its emissary had thrown her into a sudden panic. *I cannot reconcile myself to what I have become*, she thought mournfully. *I am the concubine of an Arab Sheik. How am I to look an Englishman in the eye?*

Chapter 9

Like a caged lion, Elizabeth paced the tent until darkness fell over the camp. Dressed and coiffed, her ears pricked at every sound that might indicate the return of the Sheik and signal her meeting with the Englishman she dreaded to face.

At last they came. Elizabeth made a futile attempt to calm her fluttering nerves by sitting sturdily in a chair and clasping her hands tightly in her lap. The flap of the tent flew open and two men burst in, awash in a tide of laughter and talk. Upon spotting her, the stranger immediately restrained himself and approached with a bow.

"Miss Elizabeth, I presume?" offered the stranger, bending low. Elizabeth stood and dropped a small curtsey.

"Mr. Bingley," she acknowledged.

The stranger straightened and looked into Elizabeth's eyes with an expression full of curiosity. His interest, though blatant, could never have been construed as rude. Rather, he studied her as he might have a piece of art, admiration and intrigue evident in his gaze.

Charles Bingley, it must be admitted, was a very handsome man. Far from the elderly gentleman Elizabeth had envisioned as the author of so many impressive volumes, he was instead young and energetic, his abundant energy contributing significantly to his appearance of extreme youth. He could not have been further from resemblance to his sister. His face was open and expressive, and his complexion light, if a bit sunburnt. A mass of tawny curls sprung untamed from his head, and his grin was lopsidedly contagious. Elizabeth found herself smiling despite herself.

"I am delighted to make your acquaintance," Mr. Bingley affirmed, grin broadening in response to Elizabeth's smile.

"Likewise," replied Elizabeth. Sneaking a glance at the Sheik's stern countenance, she continued: "You must be famished from your journey. Are you ready to dine?"

"Nothing would give me greater pleasure," grinned their guest.

Ringing the bell, Elizabeth was amazed to witness the prompt appearance of a small Frenchman so like Gaston that she blinked in surprise. Recovering herself, Elizabeth quickly realized that this must be Henri, brother to Gaston and valet to Mr. Bingley.

"Will you please prepare for dinner?" Elizabeth ordered gently. With a low bow, the valet retreated. Moving to the sideboard, Elizabeth poured out three glasses of strong Arab wine.

"Thank you," said Mr. Bingley, taking his glass from her hand. "Wonderful stuff, this," he continued. "But I cannot say it compares to a fine English port."

"There you are wrong," argued the Sheik, leaning forward to take his glass. "The English know nothing of liquor."

"Say what you will, Ahmed!" laughed Bingley. "But I happen to know that you shall not refuse the bottle I have secreted in my luggage for you."

At this the Sheik merely grinned and took a generous swallow of his wine.

Seating herself gently near the men, Elizabeth forced herself to join the conversation despite her shyness. "Have you been in this country long, Mr. Bingley?"

"No indeed, Miss Elizabeth," he replied. "I have been residing for the past two months in Hertfordshire, where I have taken a charming house in the country. My only wish is that Ahmed would deign to come see it! But he stubbornly refuses to step foot in the Kingdom."

"Why should I," interjected the Sheik, "when my friend will come visit me here? I cannot abide the dark skies of England, and much prefer to see the sun each day."

"Ahmed, my friend," sighed Bingley. "You take advantage of the fact that your camp is my favorite place to write. Someday, though, you will come to Hertfordshire, for it has many charms of its own."

"If I know you, Charles," teased the Sheik, "the charms of Hertfordshire all wear their golden hair in curls."

"You cut me to the bone!" cried Bingley in mock pain. "But

Ahmed...I cannot stay away for long. I have met the lady of my dreams. She is an angel, fallen from heaven."

"I have heard this tune before," moaned the Sheik.

"But not this particular chorus," retorted Bingley, raising his glass. "For she is the one!"

"I'll believe it when you ask me to stand up with you."

"Then believe it. I intend to offer for her as soon as I return to Hertfordshire."

"What recommends her, aside from her golden curls?" asked the Sheik. "They *are* golden, are they not?"

"Like sunshine."

"You have not answered my other question," prodded the Sheik, setting his glass down.

"She has much to recommend her," enthused Bingley. "She is the sweetest-natured girl I have met in my life. She is caring, and kind, and modest. Her conversation is superb. She is stunning in face and figure. What else does she need?"

"What are her connections? Her dowry?" asked the Sheik seriously.

"None to speak of," replied Bingley cheerily.

"On which front?"

"Why, both!"

"Bingley, do not tell me she is a servant."

"Do not be ridiculous, Ahmed," answered Bingley, finally sobering his tone. "She is a gentleman's daughter, the eldest of five sisters. The estate is entailed, but they have two uncles in respectable trade, one in the nearby village of Meryton and one in London."

Elizabeth's mind immediately reeled at the description. Was it possible...? Only one of her sisters had golden hair—her beloved Jane.

"Have you told Caroline about her?" pressed the Sheik, ignorant of Elizabeth's turmoil.

"I wrote to her, but her reply ignored my raptures and devolved into a plea for me to come see her, and you. You do not think she disapproves?"

"I think she does, and I am inclined to agree with her."

"Come now, Ahmed. When you meet her—"

"I hope I never shall," interrupted the Sheik. "It is plain to see that her mercenary family put her comely face before you in order to improve their own circumstances. What assurance has she given you of her love?"

"It is written in every smile, every look. She does not need to say it."

"There you have it. She does not care for you."

"She is modest!" protested Bingley.

"You would be wiser to stay here and write," said the Sheik with an air of finality. "Am I to understand that you have made no promise to this girl—what is her name?"

"Jane," said Bingley, forming the word with longing and grief. Elizabeth's heart sank at the confirmation of her suspicions.

"You have made no promise to Jane?"

"Nothing explicit, no, but we understand one another—"

"Jane does not love you any more than she loves me, Charles," stated the Sheik, ignoring Bingley's wince. "She is after your money.

You will thank me, when the image of her pretty face fades from your mind and you are able to see clearly again."

"Excuse me," interrupted Elizabeth, nearly knocking her chair over as she stood suddenly. "I have just developed a most dreadful headache. I think I will retire early."

Both men seemed to recall Elizabeth's presence at the same time.

"Forgive me, Miss Elizabeth," said Bingley, a stricken look on his face. "I am afraid we delved into much too personal a subject for mixed company. Please, do not go. My rudeness shall not be repeated."

"Indeed, Sir, you take too much upon yourself. My pain is hardly your fault." Elizabeth shot a meaningful look at the Sheik, who seemed not to notice the hatred in her gaze.

"The wine, then?" offered the Sheik innocently.

"Perhaps," she conceded.

"Then you should eat something," said the Sheik triumphantly. "You must stay for dinner."

"I beg you would excuse me," managed Elizabeth. Without another word she walked quickly to the bedroom and closed the flap behind her.

After a moment the muted sound of voices reached her ears. It sounded as though they were arguing, but then the tone became cheerful once more. Laying her cheek down on the bedspread, Elizabeth closed her eyes and thought of Jane. She could see it now. Mr. Bingley had moved into the neighborhood, probably leasing the long-vacant Netherfield estate. He had met with her family at the Meryton assembly rooms, perhaps, and asked Jane to dance.

- The Sheik of Araby -

From what little she had seen of Mr. Bingley, it was evident that he and Jane would get along famously. She did not doubt that Jane had quickly come to love him. Her sister would never show affection or give attention where no love existed; her very nature forbade it. No, Jane was in love with Mr. Bingley. That much was certain.

Mr. Bingley, anxious to gain the approval of his closest friend, had come to the Sheik of all men.

And the Sheik had destroyed all of Jane's hopes in one fell swoop. Elizabeth could hardly credit that Mr. Bingley would venture to marry against the vehement disapproval of his closest friend.

Pounding her fist into the pillow, Elizabeth cursed his name once more and laid her head down. Numbed by the stress of the day and the strong Arab wine, she fell quickly into a deep sleep.

Elizabeth woke to the sound of low voices. In a moment she realized that she was still fully dressed, her hair falling about her face as it worked its way out of its pins. Sitting up, she made a vain attempt to smooth her dress, but the silk was wrinkled beyond help. Shakily she stood, observing from the clock that it was two in the morning. The Sheik was still without.

Moving softly to the flap that separated the two rooms, Elizabeth found herself able to make out the conversation on the other side. Rapidly regaining her alertness, she put her ear to the cloth and shamelessly eavesdropped on the two friends.

"She is beautiful, to be sure, Ahmed," Bingley was saying, voice slurred somewhat by drink.

"Not only beautiful," replied the Sheik. "She has a fire within her. I have never wanted a woman so much in my life."

"Then why are you here with me? She is in your bed."

"You know very well, Bingley." The Sheik's voice was brusque. "I have my reasons to believe that to take her, as I so wish to, would harm her irreparably."

"That has never stopped you before."

"No other woman has captivated me as she does. Besides, she is English."

"I had noticed. Why abduct her at all, Ahmed, when you profess to despise the English with a vow of blood?"

"I could not resist her."

"It is the worse for her."

There was a long pause. At last, the Sheik spoke. "I know."

"I will be honest with you, Ahmed. As angry as you seem to be about Jane, I am with you about Elizabeth."

"What objection can you possibly have? You know what I am."

"No other woman was English, Ahmed. You cannot comprehend the effect this experience will have on her. She will not survive when you toss her away."

"Then she will have to stay."

"You know that is impossible. She is miserable."

"How could you possibly tell?"

"Ahmed, please! It is written on her face as plain as day. It is even evident that you have not yet touched her. She has the look of a gazelle that has just seen a leopard in the tree above her head. She is terrified."

"I confess I did not realize her discontent was so plain to see."

"Please, my friend, allow me to take her back to England with me. My word should be enough to quiet the gossips, and soon her misadventure in the East will be a memory known only to her."

"Do you really expect me to hand her over to you, Charles?"

"Is this your Eastern jealousy, Ahmed? Surely you can see that it would be for the best!"

"You admit yourself that she is lovely beyond compare. It must be my Eastern jealousy, for I will be watching you carefully."

"There is no need," replied Bingley resignedly. "I only hoped that you would see beyond yourself for once. Besides, my heart belongs to another."

"You forget that I have seen beyond myself on that very subject. It was disinterested concern that prompted my opinion regarding your Hertfordshire lady."

"You deny that the prospect of my settling permanently in England had anything to do with it?"

The Sheik's tone turned playful. "You've seen through me, Bingley. Marry *me*, my darling, and stay forever!"

"I am in no mood for your jokes, Ahmed. I will think on your advice, but promise nothing. You do not know Jane."

"If I did I would say the same. Will you never learn to guard your heart, Bingley?"

"I hope never to guard it as you do yours. Go to your English-woman. I will see you tomorrow."

Elizabeth, realizing that her position was about to be compromised, scuttled quickly to the dressing table and made as though she were letting down her hair. The rustle of the flap did not come, however, and she was fully undressed and back in bed before the Sheik made his appearance.

"I know you are not asleep, Elizabeth," he said, seating himself at the edge of the bed. In reply, Elizabeth turned over and opened her eyes. The Sheik continued. "I am most disappointed in your behavior tonight."

"I apologize for retiring so early, Sir."

"Until then you were the perfect hostess. What happened?"

"A sudden headache."

"I daresay," replied the Sheik mockingly. "But tell me, Elizabeth, why your head began to hurt."

Courage rising, Elizabeth replied honestly but understatedly. "I felt that you were unfair in your assessment of Mr. Bingley's situation."

"Am I to believe that you have faith in this lady's veracity, even though you have never seen her?"

"Though I do not know the precise nature of the lady's feelings for Mr. Bingley," answered Elizabeth truthfully, "you give your friend too little credit, both in his discernment and in his not insubstantial charm."

The Sheik twisted around, and Elizabeth felt as though he were grasping her tightly even though he had not touched a hair on her head. "You seemed charmed enough, until he mentioned his sweetheart. Never forget that you are my property, pretty thing. Shall I gift you to Bingley? I suppose you would be only too happy to distract him from his golden-haired angel."

Elizabeth's eyes blazed in defiance. "Even if you did, he would not lay a finger on me."

"And what exactly have *I* done to you, Elizabeth?" demanded the Sheik. "I could have your body at any moment, you know."

"So take it!" cried Elizabeth. "I wish you would ruin me and have done with it, so that I may leave this place!"

With fire in his eyes the Sheik grasped the hem of his linen shirt in both hands and peeled it from his body, never breaking Elizabeth's gaze. In the soft candlelight his torso shone golden, sculpted like that of a Greek statue. He turned his broad shoulders and reached a muscular arm towards her, his hand twining in the hair at the back of her neck, pulling her toward him. In a swift motion he had rolled on top of her body, weight supported by his free arm but still a crushing force. Gasping for breath, Elizabeth parted her lips.

His mouth came down upon hers with brutal passion. Her head was caught up in his hand as he drew her to him in unmistakable hunger. The painful pressure, still yet soft, of his lips upon hers exploded in a wave of sensation that threatened to overwhelm Elizabeth's very consciousness. The kiss was long and deep, seemingly unending, and Elizabeth could not have told with certainty whether it was seconds or minutes that had passed.

At last he broke the kiss and pulled back, dark eyes turned black with desire. He searched her face, deciding at last that her predominant emotion was curiosity. And so it was. She was fascinated by the spectacle of his strong, incredibly male body above her, with the pleasurable force exerted by his hips against hers. With a moan more like a growl, the Sheik moved his hand from her neck, running it down between her shoulder blades to her back. It took a moment before Elizabeth realized that he was pulling down the silk of her robe, baring one shoulder and the curve of her breast. His hand slipped around to her side, finding the breast at once and gently caressing the underside, still covered by silk. Elizabeth watched, rapt, as the silk slid over the mound of her dusky nipple and exposed it, inhaling sharply at the flash of ecstasy that pierced her brain as the seam grazed the sensitive flesh.

With a grimace of pleasure, the Sheik observed her reaction and risked running his roughened thumb over the rosy island. Currents of pleasure surged through Elizabeth's body, seeming to draw tight a string between her breasts and the pit of her stomach. At once her mind was on that sensation, a building of energy deep inside her. She felt blood rush to the spot between her legs, felt the flesh ache in a way she had never known. The pressure of his hips upon hers instilled in her only one primal desire: the urge to lift her hips into his. Feeling her slight motion the Sheik growled again, this time lowering his lips to her neck and kissing the delicate flesh of her throat. Soon his kisses moved lower, beginning to mount the hill of her bosom. Waves of stimulation coursed through her body, and her mind began to sink into pure physical response.

"Stop," she heard a voice say, only moments afterward recognizing it as her own. Instantly the spell was broken. They did not move. His weight still pressed on her, his lips still touched her breast, but all was still. The silence was deafening.

The moment passed too quickly before the Sheik's form rolled quickly off of her and to a standing position by the bed. Scooping his shirt into his hand, he muttered "I won't be back tonight," and exited the room.

Gasping for air, Elizabeth stared at the ceiling. The drapery above her head seemed to have turned a darker shade of red since the last time she had seen it, and she closed her eyes in an attempt to clear her head. Slowly she brought a shaking hand to her bared bosom, felt the goose-pimpled flesh still slick with his kisses. Rolling to her side, she turned her back to the door and drew her legs up to her chest. Toes curled beneath the coverlet, she replayed their few moments of contact over again until sleep was kind enough to take her.

- Lavinia Angell -

Chapter 10

F or the next seven days, Elizabeth was busied from dawn to dusk by the captivating presence of Mr. Bingley in the camp. As she had promised, Elizabeth played hostess to the two men, joining them for meals and seeing to their satisfaction at the table. Between repasts, the men took her own entertainment into their hands, accompanying her on long rides into the desert or including her in their friendly after-dinner conversation.

For Elizabeth, the difference in her life was as night and day. The Sheik's effervescent guest truly brought out the best in him, and his abrupt and joyful laughter became a familiar sound. The two men's camaraderie was apparent from the first, and Bingley did his best to include Elizabeth in the conversation. He never mentioned Jane again, however, and Elizabeth could not make out that he had any inkling that he was in the company of her sister. Each time Bingley alluded to Hertfordshire a cloud crossed Elizabeth's face, reminded of the pain and uncertainty her dear sister was undoubtedly suffering in his absence, which grew longer by the day. In those moments she hated the Sheik more than ever for his overreaching and arrogant influence over his friend. What right had he to dictate in what manner his friend was to be happy? Truly, he was the most unabashedly selfish man she had ever met.

His possessive nature was still wont to rear its ugly head as well. Although he had not entered her bedchamber since the night of Bingley's arrival, the Sheik's intensely attentive gaze showed that he persisted in considering Elizabeth to be very much his own personal property. If Bingley paused an excursion to point out an appealing vista to her, the Sheik would invariably break up the *tete-a-tete* with a sharp remark or even a veiled insult to his friend. Elizabeth was offended for Bingley's sake, but saw that their guest shrugged off the Sheik's temperamental outbursts with characteristic affability. Still, Elizabeth refused to be cowed into submission, and listened attentively to their guest whenever he spoke to her, even going out of her way to draw him out. The more she spoke with Bingley, the more certain she was that he was perfect for Jane. The Sheik's forbidding gaze fell often on Elizabeth and Bingley engrossed in the easy conversation for which he seemed to lack the talent, and neither could remain unaware of his disapproval. Elizabeth defied him joyously. She knew herself to be in no danger from Bingley. His regard for her was clearly platonic, as was hers for him; he seemed the brother she had never had. His every expression and gesture showed respect for her thoughts and opinions as he solicitously extended his influence to improve her mood. The Sheik was a different matter entirely.

One night after dinner the trio lingered at the table, Bingley's illicit bottle of port open and poured.

"Pray tell, Mr. Bingley, do you always bring a gift of liquor for your heathen friend?" Elizabeth asked archly, raising her glass to the light.

"Always," replied Bingley, grinning. "Ahmed will never admit it, but English port is the last vestige of Britannia that he will abide. His love in this case burns stronger than his hate."

"An interesting exception to choose!" observed Elizabeth, glancing at the Sheik. He met her gaze with calm disapproval, a characteristic frown appearing on his face. Turning back to Bingley she added, "But surely you must count yourself among his concessions."

"I hope so!" cried Bingley. "If not, then I have been sorely mistaken these fifteen years."

"Well, Sir," Elizabeth challenged, meeting the Sheik's level stare with a defiant one of her own, "though you claim to hate all things English, I am surprised to find you sitting very affably with two children of the land, speaking her tongue and enjoying her port wine. I am at a loss to account for it."

The Sheik placed his glass carefully on the table and regarded the faces of his companions. Elizabeth's countenance was open and ready to spar, but Bingley's frown showed his greater knowledge of his friend. The Sheik was unused to being questioned in this manner.

"The source of my hatred, Elizabeth," he said slowly, "is of little interest except to those concerned. I will say, however, that it was established by a betrayal that occurred some years after my friendship with Mr. Bingley was formed. Also," he continued with a wry smile, "some years after the inception of my friendship with port."

Elizabeth smiled in acknowledgment of his humor, but remained dissatisfied with his answer. It did, however, explain his perfect command of the language.

The Sheik picked up his glass once more and took a swallow, finishing it. The glass came back down as the Sheik pushed his chair away from the table.

"You are no doubt tired as well, Bingley," he said, the statement clearly a command rather than an inquiry.

"Of course," answered Bingley. "We have an early start tomorrow. Good night, my friend."

The Sheik made a formal salaam in response and left the room.

"Finish your port at least, Mr. Bingley," insisted Elizabeth, seeing his glass still half-full.

"As you wish, Miss Elizabeth," he smiled weakly, downing the rest of the liquid in two gulps.

"Must you retire at his command?" asked Elizabeth irritably, still quite awake and upset at the imminent loss of her entertaining companion.

"If Ahmed had actually commanded me just now, we would no longer be friends."

"I find that surprising, Sir. I have encountered no one yet whom he does not consider to be under his sway."

110

"Sway, perhaps," conceded Bingley, "but command, no. I am cooperating, however, because Ahmed merely wished to avoid the unseemliness of asking you to retire."

Elizabeth flushed brightly, words unnecessary to communicate her embarrassment.

"I beg you, do not take offense," added Bingley quickly. "However indelicate it may be to mention it, I know that Ahmed does not—er—share your bed. Despite that, he felt it necessary to spare your sensibilities tonight, but was unwilling to simply retire himself and leave the two of us alone."

"That's ridiculous!" cried Elizabeth. "There's no reason on earth why we shouldn't *talk*. I've been alone with him enough to ruin a thousand reputations."

"I agree, of course," admitted Bingley. "But Ahmed was merely doing what he thought best, in sacrificing a small piece of my dignity for a large share of yours."

Elizabeth stared at her hands.

"Right or wrong, his intentions are good, Elizabeth," Bingley said, placing his hand on hers. He gave it a quick squeeze before pushing away from the table and standing himself. "I should go. Ahmed trusts me, but his blood runs hot. I'd wager a pound that he's waiting for me outside."

With a sad smile Elizabeth bade him goodnight.

- Lavinia Angell -

Chapter 11

T he next morning Elizabeth woke late, head clouded by the unfamiliar effects of port. Forcing herself to sit up, Elizabeth put her hand to her head as a wave of pain shot through her skull.

"Good morning, Madame," chirped Zilah pleasantly. The girl was crouched at the far end of the room, brewing Arabian tea.

With a pang Elizabeth recalled that she was unsure how much time had passed since the startling day that Gaston had brought black native tea with her breakfast, marking the end of her planned month in the desert with stark finality. He never mentioned the change, but Elizabeth had eventually grown accustomed to the unfamiliar brew. This morning, however, was another matter.

"Coffee this morning I think, Zilah," she managed, reclining once more to a less-painful supine position.

Silently Zilah slipped from the room and returned with a pot of brewed coffee, now gone cold. Humming softly, she set it in the place where the tea had been to warm it.

That must be the Sheik's morning coffee, Elizabeth thought.

"Has your master left camp already?" she asked idly.

"Hours ago, Madame," replied Zilah. "He and Monsieur Bingley left at break of dawn."

Elizabeth knew that despite their week of pleasurable company, the two friends had planned an excursion alone to the far Western reaches of the Sheik's territory in order to conduct some sort of research for Mr. Bingley's next book. Elizabeth had not been invited, and she never asked to come along. *Just as well,* she thought. I'm no company even for myself at the moment.

One cup of strong coffee and a light breakfast later she felt much more refreshed. Pushing her heavy curls from her forehead and pinning them back, Elizabeth dressed quickly and walked out into the sunlight.

With assured strides she made her way to the tent that Zilah and Yusef now made their home. Yusef lounged outside, idly cleaning his pistol with a wooden stalk wrapped in camel hair.

"Madame," he acknowledged, bowing his head.

"I desire air and light," Elizabeth stated in her best Arabic, much improved since Ahmed had taken it upon himself to expand her vocabulary. "Monseigneur is away, so I cannot ride. I wish to walk."

Yusef looked at Elizabeth thoughtfully, evidently weighing his role as acting leader of the camp carefully. He seemed to determine that Elizabeth could not be so foolish as to attempt an escape on foot, and nodded his head once more. "Do not go far."

Leaving the camp was strange at first, familiar sights and sounds fading into the distance at such a slow pace that the separation was less freeing than frightening. On a horse, one was suddenly in the open desert. On foot, each heavy tread in the sinking dunes marked another foot that must be placed to return to safety. Resolving not to look over her shoulder at the receding camp, Elizabeth mounted the nearest dune with aching slowness. At the top she stopped to catch her breath, the wide vista of the unending desert played out before her in all its dangerous majesty.

From the top of the dunes a distant shard of rocky outcropping beckoned its promise of shade. Skipping down the far side of the dune, Elizabeth made her way to the craggy rocks, arriving out of breath and drenched in sweat.

Unbidden, memories of skipping down the path from Oakham Mount at home placed themselves before her mind. Tears sprang to her eyes as she surveyed the landscape before her, so utterly alien in its aspect. And yet, it too had a beauty all its own. Though no green farmlands or winding roads could be espied from her current vantage point, the simple starkness of the desert held its own unfathomable allure. The sheer vastness dwarfed her and made her know herself. At that moment the image of the Sheik came to her, a memory of his tall form enveloping her, of his black eyes staring into her soul.

And, at that moment, Elizabeth realized that she never wanted to be parted from him.

- Lavinia Angell -

Tears ran down her face as she wept in earnest mourning for herself. Sliding down to a crouch by the wall of desert rock, she put her head in her hands and sobbed. In the solitude of the open desert, Elizabeth thought of her future and found that she could not make herself see Longbourn, Hertfordshire or even England. All she saw was the Sheik. His eyes, his startling smile—the scent of Turkish tobacco that lingered on his snow-white robes. His damnable pride. His ridiculous arrogance. She even loved his jealousy.

At once, she vowed never to tell him that he had won. That she loved him, body and soul. His cruel words echoed in her ears. He would make her care for him, and then he would toss her away—as he had others before her.

Allowing a choking sob to escape her lips, Elizabeth brought her hand to her heart, felt the clenching pain there at the thought of the Sheik. How can I love this man? she asked herself in desperation. I have learned that he is more than he seems, but he will never love me as I deserve to be loved. To him I am an object, something to be stolen, kept, tossed away as he pleases. Elizabeth knew that the only way to keep him at bay was to hide the love that overwhelmed her soul. He could never know that he had broken her as he might one of his magnificent Arabian horses. In all likelihood, she had required less effort even than that to conquer.

Likely enough he would never touch her. Perhaps one day soon he would tire of her. But from this day to that, she would awake each morning to see his face. They would breakfast together. They would ride together. They would talk of books and philosophy before retiring. He would be stubborn and pig-headed. She would take offense at his arrogant presumptions. He would never know she adored him. She would never know why he'd kept her as long as he had.

Dusting herself off and pulling herself to her feet, Elizabeth dried her eyes and replaced her helmet. It was time she headed back. As she surveyed the desert one last time before retracing her own footsteps dimpled in the sand, Elizabeth's heart clutched in her chest. She had not seen or heard him coming, but he was a mere twenty feet away and moving quickly. A towering Moor plunged through the sandy plain towards her, and Elizabeth did not allow herself even enough time to gasp in fear before spinning and running as fast as her legs could take her toward the top of the dune that separated her from camp.

Sand caught against her feet, slowing her in an infuriating pull. The top of the dune seemed close, but certainly too far at the rate she was able to run. Sinking deep with each step, Elizabeth dared not look behind her. She had seen in that single glance the dark robes, the unsheathed saber, the murderous eyes of the dark-skinned marauder. There was no sound to either's steps, so Elizabeth had no idea how much he had been able to gain on her.

Before she realized she was toppling Elizabeth's face was in the sand, the Moor's strong hand wrapped around her ankle. She opened her mouth to scream, but sand came in and no sound came out. Frantic, she kicked at the Moor's body with her free leg. Some blows swung wide and some contacted flesh; nevertheless, the grip on her ankle did not slacken.

He pulled her down the dune towards him, clutching her clothes with his other hand in an iron grip. She pounded at his hands, bruising her own, but to no avail. She found the voice to scream, but the wind carried her voice away down the dune and she knew in her heart that no one would hear her cry. An enormous black hand clasped over her mouth as he wrestled her into his grip at last, pinning her arms to her sides. Elizabeth tried to bite, but he was too strong. An instant later he brought the hilt of his saber quickly against her temple, and all went dark.

When Elizabeth woke, she was alone.

Staring at the draped ceiling of the tent, she was momentarily certain that the Sheik had managed to rescue her already and that she was safely back at camp. Too soon her hopes were dashed; the towering Moor who had captured her stood stoically near the doorway, arms folded across his broad chest. Expressionless, he observed that she had regained consciousness and left without a word.

Mouth unbearably dry and still tasting of grit, Elizabeth looked about for some source of water. The room in which she found herself was not unlike the interiors of the Sheik's tents. Heavy draperies separated rooms, and the walls were hung with fine tapestries and skillfully worked objects of wood or metal. She lay upon a low divan, but did not seem to have been molested in any way. Her clothes were intact and her hair still clung to its few loosened pins.

The flap of the tent re-opened and a veiled woman entered the room bearing a tray and teapot. She looked as though she had been beautiful once, but years and sorrow had wrinkled her face and hardened her eyes. Bright bangles circled her wrists and neck, and her eyes were darkened with kohl.

Frowning, the woman set the tray on the table in front of Elizabeth. With a gesture, she invited her to drink.

Reaching gratefully for the hot tea, Elizabeth turned to thank the woman. At that moment the flap opened again and the Moor returned. Seeing the cup in Elizabeth's hand, he crossed the room in two great strides and knocked it violently to the floor. Elizabeth could only stare, stunned, as the pool of liquid spread over the rich carpets. The Moor bent and grasped the woman's arm, throwing her unceremoniously from the room.

"Why—?" managed Elizabeth when the Moor had turned his gaze to her once more.

The Moor's eyes narrowed. Pointing to the dark stain on the floor, he then lifted his hand in pantomime of raising a cup to his lips. Then, lips firmly closed, he shook his head sternly and made to throw his imaginary cup away.

Still unsure what had just occurred, Elizabeth tried in broken Arabic to inquire why she had been brought to this place. The Moor ignored her and merely gestured to the door, indicating that she should go through first.

Elizabeth was guided to a large room. In a chair sat a figure that was all too familiar to Elizabeth. She gasped as she perceived her captor.

The Moor bowed deeply to the man and pushed Elizabeth towards him. Ibraheim Omair sat ensconced on a cushioned dais. Next to him, the woman who had brought Elizabeth the tea lounged on soft cushions at his feet. The look in her eyes was hatred itself as she watched Elizabeth's approach.

Once she was nearly next to the dais, Elizabeth felt herself pushed to the floor by the Moor. On her hands and knees, Elizabeth stared at the floor for a long moment, unsure what to do. A loud laugh rang out alone in the quiet of the large room.

"Months, and he has still not taught you to bow," chuckled Omair. Elizabeth's cheeks flushed as she realized to whom he must be referring. "Let me see you."

Elizabeth stood.

"My uncle—" Elizabeth began.

Omair's smile broadened. "Mr. Gardiner will never see his goods, I am afraid. I have found that a very small amount of respectable work is needed to justify a lost shipment as an anomaly. Besides, I was grievously wounded in your defense."

"My aunt and uncle trusted you. I trusted you."

"And I will be trusted again," replied Omair. "It is the simple secret to my continued success."

Elizabeth dropped her gaze to the floor.

"My wives are correct to be jealous," Omair simpered, eyes taking in every curve of her form. The woman's grip on the arm of the Sheik's chair tightened. "I had nearly forgotten how lovely you truly are."

Bowing low, the Moor uttered a long sentence in an even tone. Elizabeth understood nothing of the quickly-spoken Arabic. Omair laughed again.

"I am informed that you narrowly escaped death at the hand of my first wife not five minutes ago," said Omair. "Your stupidity is not unexpected. Ahmed has lowered himself in choosing you, it seems. But then, our taste has always been similar. This is not the first time we have crossed each other over a woman, as you must know."

Elizabeth's face reddened again at the mention of the Sheik's name. Omair curled his fingers into a fist, smiling viciously.

"You blush at his name," he observed, disbelieving. "You are unplucked still!"

Unable to meet Omair's gaze, Elizabeth stared at the floor.

"That shall be quickly remedied," he continued. He reached for Elizabeth's hand. "Come here."

Before another word could be uttered, Omair's wife sprang from her seat and threw herself onto his lap, desperate words pouring from her lips. She kissed his hands and tore at her hair, but he was unmoved. At last she threw her arms around his neck, but stiffened suddenly as soon as the motion was completed. She fell away from him, eyes wide, a jewel-encrusted dagger sunk to the hilt in her breast. As she gasped her last on the floor at his feet, Omair wiped his hands on his embroidered sash, spreading a crimson swath against the golden threads. At a flick of his wrist, the Moor grasped the woman's lifeless arm and dragged her out of the room.

Stunned speechless, Elizabeth could only stare at the trail of blood that scarred the floor like a wound between the dais and the door.

"Only her jealousy could make her less attractive than her wrinkled skin," he said calmly.

"She was—your wife!" Elizabeth gasped.

"She loved me for many years," said Omair, smiling again. "You could do the same."

"Never," Elizabeth said fiercely. "Ahmed will not allow this."

The horrible laugh rang out again.

"Your Ahmed may like you very much, but he will not risk war. Especially not for a woman he does not find attractive enough to deflower himself."

Flushing with anger, Elizabeth clenched her fists. Omair continued, seemingly oblivious to the effect of his words on his captive.

"Since he had the audacity to take you from me, Ahmed has been very careful with you. By my good fortune, he was too distracted by his friend this morning to provide for your protection. It gives me great pleasure to think of his anger when he knows of your fate."

"Your deceit knows no bounds, Sir," Elizabeth said with fury.

"I did once claim honesty with you, did I not?" replied Omair, smiling. "But a promise made to a woman is the same as none at all."

"Indeed," said Elizabeth. "Zilah paid a price in blood for her trust in you."

"Zilah!" cried Omair. "So she lives still! She was such a pretty little thing, once. No doubt Ahmed took his fill of her long ago, however. Is she old before her time?"

"He never touched her," replied Elizabeth defiantly. The room echoed with Omair's laugh.

"Which of them told you that?" he cackled. Elizabeth blushed fiercely.

Amusement fading, Omair became serious once more.

"Allow me to prove that I am the monster Ahmed says I am. Your new clothes are in your room. If you do not return in five minutes wearing them, my Moor will sever one of your fingers for your disobedience."

Shaking with rage and fear, Elizabeth turned and ran back to the room from which she had come. Sure enough, a suit of small clothes lay waiting on the divan. An embroidered vest, barely long enough to cover her breasts, and a pair of harem pantaloons of a sheer material no heavier than net. Touching the articles hesitantly, Elizabeth thought of her first awakening in the Sheik's tent those months ago. So similar, and yet so different.

"Ahmed," she whispered softly, almost choking on the name. And then louder, a plea: "*Ahmed, come!*"

- Lavinia Angell -

Chapter 12

Elizabeth could see no other alternative. Sobbing, she managed to dress herself in the clothes provided but refused to alter her appearance in any other way. Her hair was a tangle of wind-knotted curls and her face and hands were smudged with desert dirt. Touching a finger tentatively to her temple, Elizabeth winced and pulled it back smudged with blood. No doubt Omair would find her disarray perversely appealing.

Elizabeth strained her ears for the sound of any approaching rescue, but was disappointed by silence. Stomach knotted, she stepped back into Omair's chamber.

"Approach," leered Omair.

Heart resisting every step, Elizabeth complied.

"Bow, woman," he commanded. Elizabeth gathered the courage to look him in the eye, unmoving.

"On your knees!" he cried, lashing out his foot in such a sudden motion that Elizabeth was caught off guard. The blow struck her shins full force, forcing her knees to buckle as she fell to the floor. Omair laughed heartily at the sight.

Before she knew it, she had been jerked roughly by the arm into his lap. Her first instinct was to leap back up but he held her fast, nuzzling the back of her neck as she struggled. The sensation of pressing against his form disgusted Elizabeth to the core, every fiber of her body resisting his tainted touch. His hands seemed to be everywhere, insinuating themselves into her most private areas. She squirmed and fought his every motion.

Just as quickly, she froze. The sharp prick of a blade against her side quashed all hope of struggle. Omair's cruel chuckle sounded against her ear as he felt her fall still. She quivered like a frightened animal as he held her to him in an unbearable stalemate.

"I think I shall have a piece of you anyhow," he whispered into her hair. "A toe will do quite as well as a finger, don't you think?"

Momentarily forgetting the blade Elizabeth lashed out, hitting his soft chin with a satisfying thud. She was free for only an instant before a heavy elbow contacted her solar plexus, knocking the wind from her lungs and leaving her gasping. In the seconds she remained helpless, Omair twisted her arm behind her back in a painful grip.

"Can you feel that?" he asked through bloodied lips.

Elizabeth nodded her head, eyes watering as she struggled to inhale.

The pain unabated, a new sensation drew her attention away from her arm. It was the unmistakable pressure of a cool blade against her skin, in the space between her two last toes.

"It would be a shame to lose one," he seethed. "But you would still be able to walk. No great loss."

Pulling her head up with an excruciating effort, Elizabeth saw the dagger at her foot move a little and a drop of blood well from the delicate skin between her toes. Pain shot up through her leg to her frenzied brain.

"*Ahmed!*" she screamed as loud as she could into the empty room, resisting her helpless state with all her might. The cry ended in a sob.

In the moments of her cry's fading echo, Elizabeth and Omair both froze at the sound of clashing metal outside the tent. A gunshot rang out, and men shouted to one another.

At first Elizabeth thought it was her imagination when she heard her name called from outside the tent. It was Ahmed's voice, tone fraught with desperation. He was coming.

"Ahmed!!" she screamed again before Omair's dagger was once more poised against her vulnerable side. A damp, fleshy hand was clamped over her mouth.

The draperies at the far end of the room parted and Ahmed Ben Hassan ran full tilt into the chamber, pistol drawn. He skidded to a halt when he saw Elizabeth in the grip of Ibraheim Omair, his knife at her side.

"*Release her!*" Ahmed bellowed in deadly serious Arabic.

"Drop your weapon or she dies," stated Omair, pulling Elizabeth tighter.

Ahmed's eyes narrowed. His gaze met Elizabeth's frantic eyes, took in her bloodied face, saw the dirt on her cheeks marred by the pale tracks of her tears.

His pistol dropped to the carpet with a muted thud.

Omair stood up on the dais, dragging Elizabeth to her feet in front of him. The pain of the knife at her side throbbed urgently, but she tried to put it from her mind. Ahmed was disarmed, helpless.

"You are a stupid boy," said Omair evenly. "But I never would have thought you so stupid as to breach my camp. Is that the sound of your men being slaughtered that I hear outside?"

Ahmed's expression was implacable. At last he took a breath and formed six slow words: "*You are going to die today.*" "Over *this?*" Omair spat, jerking Elizabeth's head back by the hair.

They were the last words he would utter. Omair had glanced at Elizabeth for a split second, enough time for Ahmed to move. Elizabeth barely noticed the cold slice of steel against her ribs as Ahmed tore her from Omair's grasp. She fell back on the dais and watched mutely as Ahmed's hands closed around other man's neck.

At first Omair gasped for air, fighting Ahmed with frenetic energy. In his leap Ahmed had managed to pin the other man's forearm against the chair with his knee and began to exert steady pressure, compressing the tendons and forcing the hand open. The dagger clattered to the dais, Omair's bulging eyes following its fall.

Elizabeth raised her terrified eyes to Ahmed's face. As he crushed the life from his enemy his expression was almost ecstatic, eyes bright and lips slightly parted in the lust to murder on her behalf. It was horrible and wondrous at the same time. Elizabeth felt that she had just seen into the Sheik's soul as she witnessed the barbarous act of killing. He was beautiful and hideous at once, and she could not tear her eyes away.

At last the choking body went limp, but Ahmed's hands took seconds longer to unclench their grip. Coming to his senses he turned his eyes to Elizabeth with an expression of intense feeling—relief, despair, desire. Their eyes locked for a long moment, a nascent understanding forming.

"Ahmed!" Elizabeth cried suddenly in warning. He spun around, ready to fight once more.

But it was too late. The Moor's glinting scimitar cut a path through the air to the young Sheik's head, where it contacted scalp and skull with a sickening crack. The Sheik fell like a stone.

Almost before the body hit the ground the Moor's eyes widened, not in triumph but in shock. A crimson gush started from just beneath his breastbone, and he touched it in disbelief before falling dead before Elizabeth's horrified gaze. She realized that the roar of blood in her ears was so loud that she had not even heard the shot.

The next thing Elizabeth knew, Bingley's arms were around her. His lips mouthed words of concern, but she was deaf to his inquiries. All she could do was reach toward the fallen form of the man she loved, saying his name over and over like a mantra.

"Ahmed – Ahmed – Ahmed – "

The hours since Bingley had leaned his ear to the Sheik's parted lips and declared that he breathed still had passed by Elizabeth in a daze. She remembered that Bingley had torn the Sheik's crisp white burnous to stanch the blood pouring from his friend's gashed head. She remembered that Yusef, gun still warm from the shot that killed the Moor, had wrapped her in a robe and lifted her like a feather in his arms. She remembered that Omair's men, on learning of their leader's death, had immediately turned on one another and allowed Ahmed's party to leave unhindered. She remembered the interminable ride back to camp, sluggish pace enforced by the body of the Sheik slumped over the saddle of his great horse Shaitan.

All these she remembered, but without emotion.

At their return the Sheik was separated from Elizabeth and taken to his tent. Bingley went with him, his education having bestowed upon him a better knowledge of medicine than any other man available. Yusef attempted to guide Elizabeth to his own tent and to Zilah, but at his urging Elizabeth found new strength to resist. Pushing him away, she trudged alone back to the Sheik's tent under his watchful gaze.

The mood was somber throughout the camp. On entering the large tent, Elizabeth's gaze went immediately to the Sheik, now laid out peacefully on the divan as though asleep.

"Miss Elizabeth," said Bingley, noticing her entry and rising from the Sheik's bedside. "I asked Yusef to take you to Zilah."

"My place is here," Elizabeth said softly. "You know that."

Bingley's countenance betrayed his recognition of the love that lit Elizabeth's eyes as she turned her gaze to the Sheik.

"Very well," Bingley allowed, expression pained at the realization of her feelings for his friend. "But you must get some rest."

"I cannot," Elizabeth managed, eyes filling with unspilled tears. "If he should—"

She buried her head in Bingley's shirt, eyes closed tight. He held her for a moment, clasping her small form as he observed the inert Sheik behind her.

"I will not pretend that his condition is not grave, Elizabeth," he said at last. She pulled away, wiping her eyes. He continued. "I have stopped the most severe bleeding and cleaned the wound. By a miracle, his skull is intact. The worry, however, is in the sharp blow to the brain. It may be bruised."

"What can be done?" Elizabeth whispered.

"Nothing, at the moment," Bingley sighed. "We will keep him comfortable and watch for signs that the brain matter may be swelling. If it does—"

"Yes?" Elizabeth prompted.

"A procedure called trepanation might be attempted as a last resort. But let us pray that it does not come to that, as few survive."

Eyes wide and serious, Elizabeth nodded her head mutely. Forgetting Bingley, she moved toward the Sheik as a moth to the flame. Taking his hand in hers, she found that she could not bear to let her eyes linger on his battered countenance. She pressed her cheek to his hand, holding his large one in both of hers. Comforted by the warmth of the tanned flesh beneath her skin, she closed her eyes.

- Lavinia Angell -

Chapter 13

E lizabeth," said the voice softly.
Elizabeth's mind rose to consciousness out of the depths of dreamless sleep.

"Ahmed," she croaked, throat hoarse and dry. She opened her eyes with effort. A hand rested upon her shoulder, but she still clutched Ahmed's hand in her own. Raising her head, she immediately brought her other hand to the sharp ache in the side of her neck. How long had she slept by his bedside?

"I am sorry, Elizabeth." It was Bingley's voice. Heart sinking, Elizabeth sat up and felt Ahmed's hand with both of hers. It was cool to the touch.

"Does he live?" she asked, panicked. The Sheik looked no different. His eyelids rested lightly on his cheeks, mouth parted slightly.

"His condition is unchanged," Bingley said quickly. "I would not have disturbed you, but – you did not tell me that you had been wounded."

Confused, Elizabeth felt timidly at her side. She winced in pain as she touched the slash of the robber Sheik's knife, incurred at the moment that Ahmed had pulled her from the monster's grasp.

"I forgot," she said blankly.

Bingley's countenance was stern. "May I—? "

She gingerly lifted the cotton robe away from the gash, grimacing as the crusted blood came away from the wound.

With tender fingers, Bingley cleaned the wound with a white cotton rag dipped in grain alcohol.

Once he was satisfied, he probed the injury gently.

"It is not deep," he said at last, wrapping a bandage around her ribs. "But we should not have waited so long to clean it. Do you feel pain anywhere else?"

Elizabeth pulled a weak smile. "Only everywhere."

"Go to Zilah," he said, pulling Elizabeth to her feet. "Change your clothes and wash. I will stay beside Ahmed."

"But—"

Bingley managed a smile of his own. "Think how angry Ahmed will be if he wakes to see you still wearing that harem outfit. Go."

Powerless to resist, Elizabeth stumbled into the bedchamber. Zilah lay on the bed, curled up in sleep. Elizabeth realized that it must be the middle of the night.

Zilah's eyes opened.

"Oh, Madame!" she cried, leaping up and throwing her arms around Elizabeth. "Are you well? You were not—you cannot have been—"

"No," Elizabeth answered, flushing. "Ahmed arrived just in time."

"Thanks be to Allah," breathed Zilah. "But the Master! He lives?"

"He breathes still," she said, eyes filling with tears at the thought of Ahmed's precarious condition.

"Allah is good," repeated Zilah, taking Elizabeth's hand in her own. "Allow me to help you."

With the tenderness of a mother, Zilah undressed her mistress and washed away the dirt and blood from Elizabeth's skin, cooing and sighing over each bruise and cut. Wrapping Elizabeth in a fresh robe, she lay her down upon the bed while she fetched a copper pot full of water and warmed it until it steamed. Then she washed her mistress' hair, rubbing away the pain in Elizabeth's head and neck with gentle caresses. Patting the mass of dark curls dry with a cotton towel, she returned Elizabeth to the softness of the bed. And then, with boldness she had never before attempted, she climbed in beside her, wrapping her arms around the broken woman.

"How did they find me?" Elizabeth whispered.

"Yusef asked me to watch you if you walked beyond sight of the camp."

"You saw the Moor take me?"

"Madame was very brave."

"I was stupid to walk so far. Ahmed warned me about his enemy to the North."

"He was an evil man," Zilah reassured her. "He was known as such by all the decent people of the desert."

"Yes," said Elizabeth, squeezing her eyes shut against the memory.

Lulled by the warmth of the room and the strength of Zilah's embrace, Elizabeth allowed sleep to pull her blissfully away from her painful reality.

It was dawn when Elizabeth returned to the Sheik's side. Grey light filtered into the tent, combating the brightly burning candles for domination of the room. Bingley slept, head thrown back, in an ornate chair pulled up to the Sheik's makeshift bed. Elizabeth clutched up a cushion from a nearby sofa and knelt upon it on the floor by the Sheik, taking his great hand in hers and kissing it gently.

"Elizabeth..."

With a start Elizabeth raised her head, expecting to see the Sheik's dark eyes focused on her. He had turned his head towards her, but his eyelids still fluttered on his cheeks. Brows drawn together in consternation, his mouth formed her name once more.

"I am here, Ahmed," she said quietly but with urgency.

The Sheik's face relaxed, but no further speech crossed his lips. Stunned, Elizabeth watched him closely for what seemed an eternity. There was no change in his unconscious state.

Half an hour passed before a growing numbness in her lower limbs necessitated an alteration in posture. Standing with effort, Elizabeth shifted her cushion and reseated herself. The movement alerted Bingley to her presence, and he raised his head with a grimace.

"Forgive me," he said groggily. "I am remiss in my vow of vigilance."

Elizabeth did not reply, rather keeping her gaze clapped on the face of their patient.

"He spoke, earlier," she said after a long moment. Bingley sat up quickly.

"Good Lord," he exclaimed. "What did he say?"

Elizabeth hesitated before answering.

"My name." Attempting to hide her hopes at the Sheik's utterance, she added: "He must have sensed that I was here."

"Indeed," said Bingley, frowning. He stood and placed his hand to the Sheik's forehead, then unwrapped the bandage from his friend's head and examined the wound. Replacing the bandage, he pulled the Sheik's eyelids gently open and held a candle to each side of his face while observing the eyes themselves closely. Elizabeth's heart sank when she saw that Ahmed's eyes, though open, held no spark of life. Bingley allowed the lids to fall closed once more and set the candle on a nearby table.

"There is no sign of swelling of the brain," he pronounced at last. "I believe the worst is past."

"He will survive?" Elizabeth asked, nearly choking on the question.

"God willing," Bingley replied gravely. "There is nothing more we can do, save let him rest. His persistent unconsciousness indicates that his body is in need of extensive repair that can only be carried out in complete stupor."

"Thank God," Elizabeth breathed. "And thank God that you are here, Mr. Bingley."

Brushing off her thanks, Bingley pushed his chair towards her. As she took the seat and reclaimed the Sheik's hand he fetched another chair from the far end of the tent.

"Ahmed and I have seen our share of scrapes," he said, seating himself a few feet from Elizabeth. "But this is another animal entirely."

"I gather that you attended school together," Elizabeth said softly. "Was he a wild youth?"

Bingley smiled. "Oh yes," he replied. "He acted as though he owned the institution—the Prince of Araby, we called him—and I followed wherever he went."

"You have a great camaraderie."

"Sometimes I feel like his younger brother," Bingley answered. "His is a personality that dominates wherever he goes, but as his friend I have been privy to moments of weakness as well. I am honored by his trust in me."

"It seems rarely bestowed." Elizabeth looked wistfully at the face of the Sheik, wishing that he might someday open his heart to her and knowing how unlikely it was to occur.

"He was much more gregarious in his youth," Bingley admitted. "Betrayal by those he once loved has made him cynical. Despite that, he is more cautious with his heart than is wise, in my opinion."

"Twice shy, perhaps," Elizabeth offered.

"Indeed," Bingley acknowledged. "I know he does not approve of my so-called impetuousness in that arena."

Bingley filled a pipe with Turkish tobacco and lit it, inhaling deeply and staring into the flame of the candle as he breathed a puff of smoke, causing the tiny light to flicker and dance.

Elizabeth gathered her courage.

"Are you thinking of Miss Bennet, Mr. Bingley?" she asked softly.

Bingley's eyes darted to her face, analyzing her expression with meticulous attention.

"I apologize again that we spoke so freely before you the night I arrived," he replied, seeing her to be in earnest. "I hope you have not been worrying that I am capricious, Miss Elizabeth."

"So you love her?" Elizabeth blushed at her own boldness, a flush that Bingley instantly mirrored.

"She is never far from my thoughts," he confessed. "But Ahmed's advice has placed doubt in my heart."

"I believe she loves you," Elizabeth said quietly.

Bingley regarded her with bemused resignation. "I appreciate your compliment, Miss Elizabeth, but I am already in possession of the kind of hopeless romanticism that you endorse. Without knowing the lady in question, your belief in her love is as speculative as Ahmed's belief in her indifference."

Elizabeth took a deep breath. "Jane would never show affection where it did not exist. Her very nature forbids it."

Bingley turned to Elizabeth in surprise. His eyes narrowed. "What are you trying to say, Miss Elizabeth?"

"Miss Elizabeth *Bennet*," she corrected deliberately.

"You cannot mean—"

"Yes," Elizabeth finished. "Jane is my sister."

Bingley leapt from his chair and took a few strides across the room, then spun to face her. Words began to fall from his lips in a jumble as pieces fell together.

"Miss Lizzy!" he cried. "When I arrived she had just departed for the East, what are the odds—Jane was so lonesome—Mr. Bennet was fearful that some ill should befall her. Her letters were cheerful. But your dark hair—fool that I am, I imagined you as a blonde, like your sister—*Ahmed!* Oh, good God!"

He covered his mouth in horror and fell back into his chair with a thud, staring into the distance for a long moment. At last he turned to Elizabeth, snatching her hands from her lap and looking her earnestly in the face. "Miss Bennet, you must know that I begged Ahmed to release you and allow you to return with me to England."

"I know," Elizabeth said quietly.

"I cannot believe this," Bingley exclaimed. "A gentleman's daughter! That *idiot!*"

Dropping his hands helplessly to his sides, Bingley took a deep breath. "God almighty, I shall never be able to face your father again. Ahmed has truly gone too far."

The weight of her position fell once more onto Elizabeth's

shoulders, and she hung her head in sorrow. It was true. The love she nurtured for Ahmed paled in comparison to the pain she would cause—and was causing—her poor family.

"Forgive me, Miss Bennet," Bingley said suddenly. "You must excuse me. I must have some time to think."

With a quick bow he stood and exited the tent, tugging at his neckcloth with frustrated jerks. As the tent flap swung closed behind him, Elizabeth returned her gaze to the unconscious form before her.

Everything revolved around him.

- Lavinia Angell -

Chapter 14

I t was some hours before Bingley returned to the Sheik's tent. He returned looking much as he had when he set out, coatless and with his shirt open at the collar.

"Good afternoon," he said, claiming his seat beside Elizabeth's. The Sheik still lay motionless.

"No change?" he asked unnecessarily.

"None," replied Elizabeth. During his absence she had dressed and styled her hair, startling him with her renewed resemblance to her sister.

"I have taken the liberty of ordering lunch from Henri," he said, seating himself lightly in his chair.

"Thank you."

"Miss Elizabeth, I feel that I must unburden myself to you," Bingley said cautiously.

"How so?"

"What Ahmed has done to you—it is inexcusable, but may be more understandable if I acquaint you with his history, a tale which only I am in a position to reveal."

"I believe I understand well enough," replied Elizabeth, lowering her eyes. "He is an Arab Sheik, and used to having his way."

"Neither, I'm afraid," Bingley countered.

Elizabeth raised her head, searching Bingley's face for some sign of humor. She found none.

"If what you say is true, then I am certain that Ahmed would not appreciate his past being laid bare. He has made no secret of his lack of regard for me."

"You may be mistaken in that too, if I am correct in my guess."

"I cannot believe that. He has told me himself that I am only one of many conquests. I am not so vain as to think myself any different."

"Very well, Miss Bennet," Bingley replied. "But I have another motive for relieving my mind. If your sister will have me, you and I shall soon be brother and sister. I cannot keep such a secret from my own flesh and blood."

Elizabeth's expression brightened. "Are you in earnest, Mr. Bingley?"

"Very much so," he answered. "I have made up my mind that Jane is the only woman for me. Whether she will forgive me for my desertion is another question."

Unable to resist, Elizabeth threw her arms around her companion, kissing him quickly on the cheek and inducing a deep flush. "I will have you know that Jane is a gentle soul with the most forgiving heart in the world. If you confess all to her, she will forgive you without a second thought."

"I hope you are right," Bingley stammered, still reeling from the impetuous embrace.

"I cannot tell you how happy it makes me that you have learned to follow your own heart in this matter."

"I am loath to confess that I was not as independent as you assume," Bingley replied. "As Ahmed and I rode out yesterday morning he informed me that he had reconsidered my situation, but reminded me of my vow to marry only where I was loved in equal measure to my own affection. His advice was for caution, but he admitted that he had been wrong to judge Jane so quickly. He even offered to accompany me to Hertfordshire in order to become acquainted with Miss Bennet himself."

Elizabeth's mouth fell open. Had her chastisement truly been taken to heart?

"Words cannot express my astonishment," she managed. "He never indicated to me that he might be swayed on this point."

"Please, Miss Bennet," Bingley entreated. "Allow me to acquaint you with our history. I am certain that you will find it most enlightening."

Overthrown, Elizabeth shook her head in defeat. "If you must, Sir."

Bingley's revelatory tale, however, was delayed by the prompt arrival of Gaston and Henri bearing the promised luncheon. Elizabeth noted with a pang the worried glance that Gaston cast at his unmoving master as he poured their tea. She opened her mouth to invite him to remain, but witnessed Bingley's redirection of Gaston's attention and reassuring look to him. Gaston's face brightened slightly, and he bowed low before taking his leave with his brother.

After only a few bites of the tempting comestibles laid before him, Bingley sat back in his chair with a cup of coffee in his hand and prepared to tell his story.

"As you have guessed," he began. "Ahmed and I met first at school – Cambridge, in fact. My own father's fortune was made in trade, but he was determined that Caroline, Louisa and I were to have the best of education. Louisa, the eldest, married shortly after her term at one of the finest finishing schools in London, and is now known as Mrs. Hurst. Caroline attended the same until her early marriage to the Vicomte de Veilleux. I studied hard and was admitted to Cambridge. Unable to conceal the fact that I was of the *nouveau riche*, however, I was at a distinct social disadvantage. Ahmed was similarly excluded, but for very different reasons. Our common social ineptitude threw us together, and before long we had become fast friends.

"I will not bore you with our adventures at school, but Ahmed came to trust me implicitly and I him. He was very lonely, you see, for the desert. During our final interval from classes he begged me to accompany him to his ancestral home. I acquiesced, and together we spent three of the happiest months of my life here at the camp of his father. My lifelong interest in the desert and its people was sparked, and I was to build much of my literary career around the advantage of my acquaintance with the intimate workings of

146

- The Sheik of Araby -

Ahmed's tribe.

"It was during that first interval that I met Ahmed's father, the great Sheik and object of Ahmed's abject worship. Since his earliest years Ahmed had striven only to make his father proud, and only for him had agreed to be sent to England to be educated despite the dreadful homesickness that depressed his spirits beyond recognition while he was there. The Sheik was adamant, however, that his young son become fluent in both English and French, as well as in the literature and history of the Western world. At his behest Ahmed did so, though in his heart all he wished for was to return to the desert and his father's side.

"As we prepared to return to Cambridge for our final term, the elder Sheik surprised me by calling me to him for a private audience. It was then that he charged me with a most terrible task, which to this day is the most painful duty I have ever been required to perform. Upon our return to Cambridge, I was to tell Ahmed that he was not his father's son. In what was perhaps the single cowardly act of his life, the old Sheik passed the task of enlightening his adopted heir to his true origins to me."

Elizabeth's hand flew to her mouth in shock, a small sound escaping her lips. Bingley sighed a deep breath and closed his eyes for a moment in memory.

"He is not the son of the Sheik?" Elizabeth gasped. "How did the adoption come to be?"

"The old Sheik shed tears as he confessed the lie to me," Bingley recalled. "Ahmed's mother was found wandering the desert by scouts of the Sheik's tribe. She was brought to the camp and nursed back to health. Even after her confusion due to exposure

147

to the sun had resolved she refused to reveal her identity, though she had been finely dressed and was evidently an Englishwoman with no command of Arabic. All she carried when she was found was a silver watch, engraved with the initials 'A.F.D.' The Sheik visited the mysterious newcomer often, and they spent many hours in each other's company. Before many weeks had passed, it became evident that the woman was with child.

"By this time, the Sheik had fallen deeply in love with the nameless lady. He begged her to marry him and allow him to give her child his name, but she refused. For five months he begged, and for five months she refused. Though she would not admit the possibility of their marriage, the Sheik assured me that she did return his love.

"By the end of this period the lady was large with child and began her labor. In the first hours of her pains, she called the Sheik to her side. Only then did she reveal her name to him – it was Anne Fitzwilliam Darcy. She confessed that her husband was master of a large estate in Derbyshire, and that they had been united to advance the fortunes of the Darcy and Fitzwilliam families. She had never loved George Darcy, whom she described as cold and distant. She had discovered her condition while traveling the continent with him and was overcome with distress at the thought of returning to England with her husband and bringing a child into their unhappy marriage, so she stole a horse and rode into the desert. The horse died of thirst, so she walked until she was certain to do the same. She had been surprised at her rescue, but could not regret it for the happiness it had yielded."

"Incredible," breathed Elizabeth. "If it could be true."

- The Sheik of Araby -

"It is most assuredly true," Bingley promised. "Mrs. Darcy knew she could not renounce her former marriage if her son was to retain his right to all that was lawfully his. She named him Fitzwilliam, for her family, and desired that on coming of age he be given the silver watch as proof of his identity when it should be needed. Weakened by the birth, she was plagued by illness from that point forward. She remained in the camp, the object of the old Sheik's unaltered affection, until her death when Ahmed was but four years old."

Tears ran down Elizabeth's cheeks as she pictured the heartbroken Sheik, left alone with the child of another man at the death of the woman he loved.

"The old Sheik was never able to bring himself to tell the boy of his sad beginnings, so he raised him as his own and made him heir to the seat of the tribe and all his worldly possessions. He knew, however, that he was bound by honor to obey Mrs. Darcy's wish and to allow the boy to claim what was his by English law.

"Having placed the burden of the truth upon my shoulders the old Sheik gave me the silver watch and a letter written by Anne for old Mr. Darcy, begging me to reveal the story to my friend once we were returned to England. I tried to refuse the charge, but the Sheik would not be gainsaid.

"I returned to England with a heavy heart indeed, which Ahmed fortunately ascribed to the loss of the desert scenery. Once back in England, I posted the letter, enclosing the watch, and awaited a reply.

"I did not wait long. Old man Darcy was effusive in his astonishment and joy that he had a son living, and wished to meet the

149

boy immediately. Unexpectedly, he also informed me that he had journeyed to Cambridge directly on receipt of the letter and awaited our visit at any time.

"I had little choice but to prepare Ahmed to meet his father. I will not go into detail regarding the painful conversation, but Ahmed did not take the news well. He was crushed—lost in anguish at the realization that his life had been a lie. He blamed the old Sheik for hiding the secret for so many years, and I believe he even harbored a strong anger against the man for not having fathered him, as illogical as that might be. Against the English landowner who had failed his mother he felt an even deeper hatred, condemning him for his mother's unhappiness and feeling that a better man would not have given up so easily on his missing wife. I admit as well that even the messenger did not escape unscathed, for I did not see or hear from Ahmed again for more than a year following the revelation.

"Ahmed refused to see Mr. Darcy, of course, and swore that he would forfeit all that was due to him at the man's death. Ahmed packed his room at Cambridge and left the country forthwith, not returning to his tribe but rather retreating in hurt and anger to an extended period of travel. I took it upon myself to visit Mr. Darcy and apprise him of his son's reaction.

"I cannot say the man was surprised, but his grief at the news was difficult to witness. He enlightened me to the fact that he had remarried many years after his wife's disappearance, and was now a widower father to a young girl of seven by the name of Georgiana. He refused to renounce his son, however, and had already altered his will to fix a dowry of thirty thousand pounds on Geor-

- The Sheik of Araby -

---

giana, leaving the rest of the estate to fall into Ahmed's hands, or Fitzwilliam's, as he called him.

"I did not hear from Ahmed again until well after I had graduated from Cambridge. The following summer I received a letter from him informing me of the death of the Sheik his father and his inheritance of the tribal seat. He asked me to visit him in his homeland, to which I agreed. Ahmed's father died before he was able to confront him about his parentage, or reconcile with him. He regrets it keenly to this day. I helped him through the first difficult months of his rule, and through the agony of the betrayal of his childhood friend, Ibraheim Omair, who attempted to murder Ahmed in pursuit of the seat of power.

"Many years have passed since the fateful moment that his world fell apart, Miss Elizabeth," Bingley continued. "I believe that each day has been a struggle for him, an agonizing choice between his heritage and his upbringing. He claims to despise all English for the crimes of his father, but in doing so he must despise himself. I do not know why he brought you here, but I suspect that it has something to do with the tale I have just related."

Elizabeth turned her head from Bingley to the Sheik beside her, viewing his placid expression through a veil of tears. He had endured so much pain, and inflicted much in turn, but she could not bring herself to hate him for it. She thought of his words on her first morning in this tent, of how he promised she would be happy. Had he wished, in the depths of his psyche, to rescue her from the same life his mother had led with her English husband?

Minutes passed in silence. At last Bingley spoke gently to Elizabeth, placing his hand on her arm.

151

"Ahmed has had—dalliances," he said softly. "From what I gather, he has informed you of such himself, and indeed it is expected of a man in his position. But you must know that these were women who went into the affairs with their eyes open. He has never acted in this manner before. To take you—kidnap you—it is unconscionable. But you and I both know what it means to challenge Ahmed's iron will. There was nothing I could do on this point save abscond with you myself, and in doing so would have acted hardly better than he."

"Did he not tell you?" Elizabeth asked in confusion. "My guide through the desert was Ibraheim Omair himself. I could not have known it at the time, but I now believe Ahmed meant to rescue me from his power."

Bingley raised his eyebrows. "Ahmed never ceases to surprise me," he said. "I knew that Omair was near, but he never mentioned your name in connection with his."

Another silence fell as both regarded the recumbent Sheik in thoughtful contemplation.

"My sister Louisa keeps house at Netherfield during my absence," Bingley said after some pause.

"I beg you would allow me to enclose a letter to your father in my correspondence with her in order to ease his mind."

Elizabeth's eyes flashed. "You would not tell him—!"

"Of course not," Bingley reassured her. "I shall merely write him that I have happened to see you during my travels, and that you are well."

Brow furrowed, Elizabeth weighed the option. "I dare not write him myself," she mused. "For there is no way to explain the time elapsed without causing him great pain."

Finally she nodded. "I thank you, Mr. Bingley. It is a good plan."

"I will not be returning to Netherfield until Ahmed's condition changes—one way or another." He skipped over the words quickly, not wishing to pain his companion. "But should you wish to go, I will see to it that you reach your home in safety."

Regarding the face of the man lying next to her, Elizabeth found that her dearest wish of mere days ago was now the last thing she desired. She could not leave without saying goodbye.

"No," she said firmly. "We will stay together. One way or another."

"Very well," Bingley replied, standing. "I shall go write my letters. Forgive me."

With a quick bow he turned and left, leaving Elizabeth and the Sheik very much alone.

"Ahmed," she whispered. "You must come back."

- Lavinia Angell -

Chapter 15

As day turned to dusk in the Arabian camp, Elizabeth relaxed her vigil somewhat and took up a book. It was difficult to focus, but the lack of movement in the body laid out on the makeshift sickbed had begun to depress her spirits. She wondered what she would do if he did not awake—and what she would do if he did.

A small movement caught Elizabeth's eye and she raised her head with a jerk. The Sheik had turned his head, ever so slightly. The book fell to the floor as she knelt by the bedside and grasped the Sheik's large hand firmly. His mouth was set in a hard line, lips pressed together as though he resisted consciousness. He turned his head away from her, then back again, limbs beginning to return to life. The strong hand squeezed hers back, flesh warm and lithe beneath her own.

"Elizabeth," he said hoarsely, eyes closed tightly. "Where is she?"

"Here, Ahmed," Elizabeth answered, breathless with hope and fear.

The Sheik's eyes flew open and his gaze pierced her very soul. Anger, desire, grief and desperation melded into one smoldering look that left Elizabeth gasping for air. He took in every detail of her face, her hair, her clothes. The hand clenched tighter until he began to crush her small digits.

At her cry the grip relaxed and the Sheik's head turned away from her once more.

"What are you doing here?" he asked, voice low with rage. He drew his hand from hers, leaving her bereft of his touch. "You should have gone back to England the moment you were freed. Bring me Bingley."

Elizabeth stood and turned away wordlessly. Though she knew she loved him still, his coldness and curt dismissal reminded her all too vividly of the coarse treatment she had suffered at his hands.

Fighting to maintain her composure, Elizabeth pulled aside the flap of the tent. As was his habit, Gaston sat in a small chair just outside the entrance in anticipation of his master's call. Henri sat next to him, a recent addition to the accustomed scene. The brothers spoke amiably.

"Good evening, Madame," said Gaston, noticing Elizabeth's emergence and making his way politely to his feet. "What can I do for you?"

Elizabeth took a deep breath. "Summon Monsieur Bingley," she said. "Your master has awakened."

With a start, Gaston exchanged surprised glances with his brother before dashing in the direction of Bingley's tent. Ignoring Henri's questioning gaze upon her, Elizabeth lifted the tent flap once more and re-entered the chamber.

Ahmed's back was turned to the door when she returned, and he showed no sign of having heard her entrance. A pain formed in her throat, spreading to an ache in her chest as she contemplated that he might refuse to see her even once more. Heart breaking, Elizabeth crossed quietly to the bedchamber, lay upon the bed and stared at the ceiling in a stunned stupor.

"How is he?" Elizabeth asked despairingly when Bingley finally entered the bedchamber, nearly an hour after the Sheik's first words.

"Physically, he is progressing well. There is no sign of harm to his mind from his wounds, and all he requires is time to heal the rest of his body."

"Has he asked for me?" she tried, attempting to push down the hope that rose in her throat. Bingley sat down wearily near her, rubbing his hand over his eyes before replying.

"I am unsure what to tell you, Elizabeth," he said with a pained expression. "He does not wish to see you."

"What do you mean?" she asked in a small voice. "Does he blame me for wandering too far? For his injuries?"

"No, no, nothing like that," Bingley reassured her. "It may be the whim of an invalid, but he has asked that he be moved to my tent, while you are to remain here."

"But that's ridiculous," she protested. "This is his home."

"I think he would rather be moved himself than ask you to move," Bingley sighed. "He would not explain further, but he was quite insistent that you were not to be permitted to see him."

Elizabeth covered her mouth with her hand, biting back the sob that threatened. This was worse than she had imagined.

"I'm sorry, Elizabeth. I know you were very solicitous while he was ill, but we must accede to his wishes now."

"Damn him!" she cried, leaping to her feet and leaning heavily on the side table. "That arrogant, selfish, unfeeling man!"

The words tumbled from her lips in unfocused fury. Bingley stood at once and placed a hand on her shoulder as she crumbled into tears. Clutching his shirt, she sobbed against his shoulder.

"Bingley!"

The Sheik's voice carried from the outer chamber, causing Bingley to start and Elizabeth to look up with red-rimmed eyes.

"Forgive me," Bingley said quickly, extricating himself from Elizabeth's grasp and crossing the room to the entry. With a final anguished look back at the weeping woman, he rejoined the Sheik.

"For the sake of Allah, Bingley, call Gaston and arrange for my transport," the Sheik's stated in frustrated tones easily audible to the listener in the bedchamber. "I cannot stand to hear her voice for another moment."

158

- The Sheik of Araby -

Seating herself on the edge of the bed, Elizabeth placed her hands over her mouth and quieted the sobs that burst from her breaking heart. Soon her body stilled, tears subsiding into the occasional hiccough. Outside the door she could hear the tumult generated by the Sheik's request. Without even a final word to her he was gone, and she was alone once more.

- Lavinia Angell -

Chapter 16

Days passed with aching languor. Every hour Elizabeth listened for the sound of Ahmed's voice, or his footstep crossing her threshold. The sound never came.

Each day Bingley visited her several times to apprise her of the Sheik's progress. One day he ate lentils, the next he sat up in a cushioned chair. Elizabeth attended with intense interest, though her eager reception seemed only to sadden the bearer of the news.

Itching for an occupation to take her mind from the man she was forbidden to see, Elizabeth requested permission to ride once more. The slash in her side was healing neatly over the course of but a few days, and a fresh bandage each day served mainly to protect the wound from the friction of her clothes against it. Her bruises and cuts were fading, and she felt presentable enough to be seen by the rest of the tribe.

Accompanied by Yusef, Elizabeth took Lujine for short jaunts into the nearby desert, never leaving sight of the camp. One afternoon as they returned to the safety of the cluster of tents, Elizabeth was shocked to see the figure of the Sheik standing at the side of the corral where the horses were kept. Riding closer, she reined Lujine in as she witnessed the moment he caught sight of her. His dark skin flushed scarlet, gaze piercing her resolve to come nearer to him. Caught in the depth of his stare, Elizabeth returned it until he broke the spell, angrily calling to one of his men and leaning upon him as he made his way weakly back towards Bingley's tent.

Driven by the emotion of the encounter, Elizabeth felt a sudden impetus to follow him and press him to explain his self-imposed exile from her company. She dismounted hastily and covered the ground between the corral and the tent with quick strides.

To say that Ahmed was surprised to see her enter the room would undoubtedly be an understatement. For the first time in her memory, Elizabeth witnessed an expression of complete shock on his face, lips slightly parted in abstraction for a split second before he regained his composure. He sat gingerly at the edge of a divan, his arm still wrapped about the shoulders of the man who had helped him walk to it. With a pointed look at Elizabeth, he issued a clipped command in Arabic that translated roughly to "Leave us."

As soon as the flap had swung closed behind the tribesman, the Sheik addressed his visitor.

"I was under the impression that you had been told that I do not wish to see you," he said angrily, eyes blazing.

"You are correct, Sir," Elizabeth countered quickly. "I have been told."

"Undermining my authority by coming has angered me greatly. You must know my nature well enough by now to expect it."

"And you must know mine well enough to suspect that I would chafe under a restriction which has no sense behind it," Elizabeth retorted. "Kindly inform me of your reasons for removing yourself from your tent and I shall be happy to return there alone."

The Sheik shifted himself back on the divan with a slight wince of pain.

"My own reasons are of no concern to you," he replied. Throughout the interview he had refused to meet her eyes, gazing rather at the carpet near her feet.

"Why will you not look at me, Sir?" Elizabeth pressed. "Am I so repulsive to you, as you once put it?"

The Sheik raised his eyes, taking in her face with a frown.

"You are by no means repellent," he sighed wearily. "But you must respect my order to stay out of my sight. Before long there will no longer be any need, but for the time being please stay clear of this tent."

"Once you are recovered, you mean?" Elizabeth asked, confused.

"Yes," he said. "Our situation will change once I am myself again."

Still unsure as to his meaning, Elizabeth could only hope that he planned to return to his own tent once he no longer needed constant attention. Perhaps an Eastern custom forbid her to attend him in his weakness. Seeing that he was growing weary, she moved to go.

"I will obey you," she said softly. "But I look forward to the day that you are well."

The Sheik closed his eyes in evident fatigue, a pained expression crossing his visage. "Endure it as best you can for a while longer," he said. "I assure you that I am gaining rapidly."

"I am glad to hear it," Elizabeth said. Turning, she exited the tent and raised her face to the beating desert sun. *Soon,* she thought, dreaming of the day that he would be beside her once more.

Fearing that she had given away too much in expressing her desire to see him, Elizabeth waited each morning for news that the Sheik was well enough to return to his own tent. She hoped desperately that he had not guessed at the love she harbored for him, dreading the fulfillment of his promise to discard her once she failed to interest him. His extended absence only confirmed her fears, and each lonely night signaled his lack of interest with painful clarity.

Upon returning from her daily ride some five days after her last glimpse of the Sheik, she was astonished upon entering the tent to see him standing in the center of the room.

"Ahmed!" she breathed.

His eyes widened. "Please do not address me so," he said coldly, regaining his composure. "It is overly familiar."

164

He looked well, standing straight and tall, though his face showed the marks of constant pain.

"Forgive me, Sir," Elizabeth replied, chastened. "It is only that I had not expected to see you."

"The day has arrived," he said sarcastically, extending his arms out in an elaborate but restrained bow. "You have no doubt been awaiting it with bated breath."

Elizabeth was unsure how to answer this strange declaration, and so remained silent. At that moment she noticed that the flap to the bedchamber was tied back and her trunks closed and stacked neatly beside the opening. Unable to resist, she tore her eyes from the Sheik and stepped forward to look into the room, which was altered without precedent.

All of her things had been cleared away. The vanity at the end of the room was bare of all her toiletries and her clothes had been folded and stowed.

"What is happening?" she asked, panic rising. *He cannot not be sending me away already,* her thoughts protested. *He cannot!*

"I have arranged for your belongings to be packed. You may of course add anything that I have given you which you might wish to keep."

She spun to face him. His face was unreadable, his eyes focused into the distance just above her head.

"You are finished with me?" she asked, disbelieving.

"Yes," he said levelly. "Now that I am recovered, Bingley shall be returning to Hertfordshire. He has apprised me of the fact that said county is also your home. He will take you safely to your family."

"When are we to depart?" she asked, feeling ill.

"At dawn tomorrow. Be ready. I shall accompany you as far as Biskra."

Without another glance in her direction, he turned his back on her and strode toward the entrance of the tent, white robes billowing about his frame.

With a jolt Elizabeth realized that she had nothing left to lose. He had tired of her, and nothing she said or did could revive his interest.

"Do you believe that I love you?" she asked. He stopped in his tracks, but did not face her.

"Of course not," he replied, voice icy. "I would be a fool to think so."

A flicker of hope entered her mind and she clutched at it. "And yet you swore that you would not let me go until I did."

He turned once more, spinning slowly on his heel as he regarded her seriously.

"If your aim is to taunt me for my failure, then claim your right. You have proved a worthy opponent."

"I am surprised to hear you admit it," Elizabeth acknowledged.

"I will concede that I have been bested," he replied. "It is clear that you hate me as much as you ever did, and deservedly so. I only regret that I was not able to free you sooner."

"And now you turn me loose, reputation in tatters, to return to my family as though nothing has happened?"

The Sheik's face darkened. He stepped forward and grasped her by the shoulders, forcing her to look him in the face.

"I will never," he said slowly and deliberately, "apologize for

166

bringing you here. Though I did wrong in abducting you against your will, the motives that prompted the action were natural and just. Could I have been expected to woo you with trivial conversation as though you were not an Englishwoman and I a Muslim Sheik? To conceal my struggles and flatter you? To rejoice in the hope of a connection so perverse in its nature, so unprecedented in its composition? Though you may never forgive me, I cannot find it in this selfish heart to regret these days with you. If that is your goal by this line of questioning, give up now."

Elizabeth stared at him, mind swimming at his admission as she took in the feel of his hands on her skin, the yearning in his countenance, the heat of his body as he stood almost near enough to touch. *Is it possible that he cares for me?* she wondered boldly.

In a sudden, desperate motion she raised her head and pressed her lips to his. She felt his grip on her shoulders tighten as he started in shock. He recoiled from her touch.

An ache formed deep inside her as she opened her eyes and saw his stunned expression. Her kiss had been the last thing he had expected. She turned her head away, unable to face his reproof.

"Why did you do that, Elizabeth?" he asked with emotion, dropping his hands from her shoulders and taking a step back.

Silent moments passed as she asked herself the same question.

"You have an uncanny ability to cause me pain," he said softly, almost to himself, fists clenching at his sides.

"Forgive me," Elizabeth managed formally, still shamed at his rejection. "It was unconsciously done, and I hope will be of short duration."

"Short duration," he repeated, scoffing, pacing a few steps

away and running his hand through his hair in frustration. "If only you knew."

"Knew what?" she challenged, ire rising at his self-pity. "That you despise yourself for failing to win me? That Bingley and Yusef will never respect your manhood after you lose me? That every other woman you have ever known gave herself to you, but the one you stole never would?"

"Yes," the Sheik replied quietly after a moment's somber reflection, eyes glinting in self-remanding disgust as he stared at the carpet between their feet. "This is the reply I should have known to expect. I have been the author of my own image, in your eyes. Your opinion of me was set at the moment you awoke in this tent. Or was it before? Was it the moment you saw me?"

"If I am incorrect, defend yourself," Elizabeth pushed.

"Whether you know it or not, Elizabeth, you have paid me back a hundredfold for the insult of your capture," the Sheik said solemnly, raising his eyes to hers. "But not because I regret my action. You pierce my heart when you look at me with disdain plain on your features. Your loveless kiss brings only memories of the anguish I have caused you. Your face bears the scars of the tortures to which I have exposed you. Your very presence here is proof of my inhumanity.

"You must go, painful though it will be to return to your family after what I have done to you. I ask you to do it, however, to take the brunt of the censure you will endure, because I am too weak to look you in the face for one more day."

Elizabeth regarded him for a moment, acknowledging the genuine strife that was evident in his voice and tensed figure.

"You wish me to go, in order to free you of the guilt you have brought upon yourself?" she asked simply.

"I beg of you to go," he confirmed, face clouded in disgrace. "I can stand only so much, and to witness the hatred in your eyes when you look at me is too much for me to bear. I cannot repress my feelings another day. I love you ardently, passionately, but you have proven that I can never have that which I want more than anything. I have learned, painfully, that I am incapable of pleasing a woman worthy of being pleased."

Stunned, Elizabeth took a moment to regard the man before her. The twisted furrows of pain on his countenance stood out in sharp relief, mouth closed in a tight line against further admission. His shoulders slumped in defeat and he grasped the sturdy back of a chair to steady his frame, weakened by injury and grief.

"I will not go," she said quietly, firmly.

He looked up in question, face contorted in anguish. "To punish my crime?" he asked.

"To love you," she replied, heart pounding against her breast.

His face showed disbelief, then pained amusement as a mirthless laugh escaped his lips, eyes full of anger.

"The pretense of your love is crueler still than the reality of your hatred," he seethed, "and to torture a man who has no hope of winning your heart is no better than what I attempted to do to you. I implore you, Miss Bennet, to go back to England and forget me, though I shall never forget you."

"My love is as real as you or I," Elizabeth said, eyes filling with tears. "But you have been too blind, too arrogant, too stupid to conceive of it! You know everything, Ahmed, do you not? Do you know the secrets of a woman's heart?"

He regarded her in blank surprise, a dawning belief slowly softening his features. Suddenly he stepped towards her once more, lifting her chin with a trembling hand and studying her swimming eyes with furious attention.

"Are you in earnest?" he whispered hesitantly.

"Yes," she wept, tears spilling down her cheeks.

He pulled her into his embrace, clutching her as though afraid that she would slip through his fingers.

"Allah has done it," he breathed. "I would not believe it, except from your own eyes. There is no woman for me but this one I hold."

Lost in the warmth of his embrace, Elizabeth wept to know that the man she loved could care for her as well, to hold her as she had always hoped to be held.

The circle of his arms slackened, and he lowered his mouth to her ear. "Kiss me again," he murmured urgently, breath hot against her neck.

She raised her lips to his. His arms wound about her waist as she kissed him gently, then with more insistent force. With a low moan he responded, pressing his mouth to hers with barely-contained need.

"I love you, Elizabeth," he gasped at last, pulling away for breath.

"Say that I will remain with you, Ahmed," Elizabeth begged, tears running down her cheeks. "I cannot bear to leave you."

The Sheik's eyes glistened as he regarded her earnest face. "You must stay with me always, and be my wife," he said firmly. "You must allow me to love you, every day from this one forward."

170

- The Sheik of Araby -

"Yes," she said, smiling through her tears. "Despite all that has happened – this place, this world, this man – you are my home."

- Lavinia Angell -

Chapter 17

How shall we be married, my love?" asked the Sheik, languidly stroking Elizabeth's hair.

They lay upon the bed still fully clothed, basking in the warmth of each other's bodies. Elizabeth was clasped in one of the Sheik's great arms, her chin nestled in the hollow of his collar bone. His large hand twined through her hair in a rhythmic motion that caused her eyelids to droop sleepily.

"Hmm?" she asked drowsily. "Oh dear, I don't know."

"We must be married in the way of my people," he said matter-of-factly, "but if it is your desire we may also be married in a Christian ceremony."

"In Biskra?"

He made a face. "I hope you will not be insulted if I refuse to let your cousin Collins marry us."

Elizabeth laughed. "Where then?"

"You will want to see your parents? If you can abide the idea of bringing an Arabian savage to their door, we could make the journey to England with Bingley."

"They will have to bear it, for I know not when we will see them after we return to the desert. I beg you, though, do not tell my mother that you have spurned your inheritance of half of Derbyshire. She will never forgive you."

"Will she be pleased with me?"

"Can you make yourself pleasant?" Elizabeth retorted. The Sheik brought his hand to his heart in mock pain.

"I am justly accused," he replied. Then, seriously: "I will do all I can to make them happy with your choice."

"My father will never be pleased."

"Of course not. You are his favorite."

"How did you know?"

"A daughter like you would be my favorite."

Elizabeth laughed lightly, eyes misting at the thought of her father.

"I love him very much. I will miss him terribly. I cannot bear to think of the pain he must be feeling—"

Ahmed took her into his arms. "Bingley tells me he has written of you in his latest letter home. Will you write to your family, your uncle? I will send my fastest riders with the messages, so that they will not have to worry any more."

"What will I tell them?"

174

"What you like. The truth, if you wish it. I deserve no special consideration for my monstrous behavior."

"I will think of something," she mused, furrowing her brow.

"There has never been a woman like you, Elizabeth," he said wonderingly.

Elizabeth was silent, mind on her family.

Sensing her thoughts, the Sheik craned his neck to look her in the eye. "It is too much? Too far?" he asked quietly. "You wish that I would accept my inheritance, that we might live in England instead?"

"Absolutely not," Elizabeth said firmly. "You would never be happy there."

"I would never be happy without you," he countered.

"Fear not," she replied. "I have come to love the desert almost as much as I love you, my darling."

"Beware, or my Eastern jealousy will raise its ugly head."

"Let it."

"You will miss your sister?"

"Very much."

"I hope that she and Bingley will visit often, then," he stated, as though the marriage he had once so vehemently opposed was an accomplished deed.

"Are you angry with him, for revealing your secret to me?" Elizabeth asked gently.

There was a moment of silence as he considered his answer.

"I am not angry," he said at last. "I was, before. I was sure that you would hate me all the more. I dreaded your knowing that the same blood ran in our veins but that I could not be the man you wanted. But now that you are to be my wife I am glad that you know my true history."

"You should be grateful to him," Elizabeth said.

"Why?"

"The knowledge of your past opened my heart to you fully. I was aware of my own love, but frightened of the man I thought you were."

"An Arab, you mean," he said stoically.

Elizabeth sat up. "Of course not, Ahmed!" she cried.

"You maintain that my heritage means nothing to you? I seem to recall that you once called my cruelty a birthright."

"I was mistaken," she said earnestly. "So very mistaken. I came to love you, you know, before I ever heard a word about your mother. I never suspected that you were anything but the son of the Sheik your father."

"Be that as it may, I still do not know why you love me, Lizzy," the Sheik said, sending a thrill through her.

"I like it when you call me Lizzy," she smiled, and was glad to see her smile returned. His expression softened into concern.

"Tell me though, Lizzy, how you can love such a brute."

"I did hate you at first, passionately," she admitted. Seeing the pain in Ahmed's face she added: "Do not tell me that you did not deserve it."

"I did, most heartily," he said solemnly.

"Do you know, I think that it was despite you that I came to know you. I eventually realized that your treatment of me was an aberration in your character. I still do not know why you acted as you did."

"The truth, Lizzy?" the Sheik asked, pulling her on top of him. Elizabeth nodded.

"I could not resist you."

She laughed and tried to roll away, but he pulled her back.

"Do not laugh," he said seriously. "From the moment I first saw you in Biskra I was enchanted by your beauty. Each time we spoke you challenged me in a way that made me ache for more. I acted on a terrible whim, bringing you here. I justified it by telling myself that it was the way of an Arab brute, and what you might expect of me. Your pain and reproof hurt me deeply, and I knew that I had been wrong as I never had before, but each time you resisted me, I wanted you more. When I admitted to myself that you would never have me I even tried to push you away, to repulse you. I fought myself, day after day, trying to convince myself that I could not love the woman I had stolen."

Her eyes softened, and she leaned down to kiss him gently. Entranced, he pulled her to him and possessed her mouth with passionate intensity.

"I thought you despised me," she said finally.

"I tried to," he replied. "I did hate you, somehow, for being so irresistible to me. Your every word, your every action seemed designed to make me want you more."

"You could have had me at any time," she said, lowering her eyes.

"Look at me," he said softly. When her gaze was once again raised to his, he continued: "I have never loved a woman with the entirety of my heart, as I do you. At the thought of physical congress—I was sure that I would never be able to let you go."

177

"You could have kept me here," she prodded.

"You know that to watch the woman I loved suffer at my hands a moment longer would have been worse than death."

"So you decided to send me away."

"Do you know," he said, "that when you were captured and taken from me by my enemy, almost surely to be despoiled, I hoped that I would die in the act of taking you back from him? I did not know how I could continue, knowing that I had brought you to that."

Elizabeth shook her head, trying to stop the words from spilling from his lips.

"You must listen," he said, holding her tight. "I was furious, at first, to find that I had lived. The first thing I asked Bingley was if you had been forced. I held a knife in my hand, secretly poised at my breast, in case the answer should be yes."

Elizabeth gasped in horror at the admission.

"Even though the worst did not come to pass," he continued placing his hand on her cheek, "I had already seen the marks of torture on your body. I knew that I had to remove you from this dangerous place. I also knew that if I saw your beautiful face, I would not be able to make myself send you away. I told Bingley to keep you from me."

"I missed you so," Elizabeth said tenderly.

"I thought I saved you pain," he replied with regret. "But I always cause it, fool that I am."

Elizabeth turned on her back, taking the Sheik's hand in hers and pressing it to her heart. He grasped it tightly, then rolled to his side so that they lay face to face.

"Please, Elizabeth," he said, holding her hands in his. "Do not leave me. I could not bear it if you should change your mind and go. I feel as though I am in a dream, that I will awake to find you gone."

"I will be here, Ahmed," she assured him gently. Nestling her head against his chest, she whispered: "I will be here."

THE END